P9-ELW-051

FALSE PREMISES

FALSE PREMISES

Winthrop Knowlton

RANDOM HOUSE NEW YORK

 Published in the United States by Random House, Inc., New York, and simultaneously in Canada by Random House of Canada Limited, Toronto.

Library of Congress Cataloging in Publication Data

Knowlton, Winthrop.

False premises.

I. Title.

PS3561.N685F3 1983 813'.54 82-21569

ISBN 0-394-53087-X

Manufactured in the United States of America

2 4 6 8 9 7 5 3

First Edition

TO MAXINE

PART
I

1

"ARE YOU SURE, darling, you won't come with us after all?"

The scene was the breakfast table of our red-brick Georgian house on the North Shore of Long Island; the time, the summer of 1939. I was ten years old, and my mother had just begun taking me on her monthly pilgrimages to the small village in southwestern Massachusetts where my Grandmother Starcliffe lived.

My father, stern, immaculate, smelling pleasantly of bay rum, raised his strong, square head from the stock market tables of his morning newspaper and stared at my mother with pale-blue eyes. When provoked, he widened his eyes in a way that seemed to drain them of color. That was the look he turned upon her now. She took a little breath and brought her hand up quickly to hold her pearls. Returning to his newspaper, my father reached into his vest pocket for a slender gold pencil with which he wrote, in a slender gold-tipped notebook, assorted symbols and sums.

"Arthur won't be there." Her husky voice was scarcely more than a whisper.

My father's pencil stopped; he despised my Uncle Arthur. Then, without looking up, he said, "Sarah, *no*."

Now she sat a little straighter and tilted her head back and viewed him as though from a great distance. I was familiar with these finely calibrated encounters. When I was present, their voices were hardly ever raised, their joustings a matter of nuanced tone and glance. I tried to explain to Mother that unless we hurried we would miss the ferry. "Shush, Peter," she said sharply, her eyes never leaving my father's face.

"*Next* time, darling? Surely you will come with us *once*?"

Not until he heard the words "next time" did my father give a little sigh; now he knew he was off the hook. His head came up; he smiled, the kind of smile in which the work is done by the mouth, the eyes not really joining in. "Why yes," he said cheerfully, "I will certainly come if I can."

It was what he said every time.

Fräulein came through the swinging doors with smelts and bacon. "More juice, Herr Kempton?" "*Nein, danke, Fräulein,*" and on he went, the pencil making its careful notations, the choreography of numbers in his head far more vivid to him than any breakfast-table drama.

My brother Randolph had explained to me what it was our father wrote each morning in his notebook: he was figuring his net worth. And that was how I pictured him after my mother and I were on our way, *fixed* there at the table, figuring this thing I didn't understand, even though I knew perfectly well that before long he would consult his watch, push back his chair and rush out to the driveway, where Tony stood, cap in hand, ready to drive him at breakneck speed ("Step on it, Tony, for God's sake!") to the Clarkstown station. And I knew that when he came home in the evening he would be exhausted and eat alone, his martini glass beside him, reports piled on the dining-room table, and after dinner he would walk over to Stim's. Through our old apple orchard and on across Stim's Great Lawn he would go, head down, deep in thought. And the two of them, my father and my godfather, Peter Stimson, would sit in a pair of canvas chairs on the lawn, sipping brandy and puffing cigars, conversing in low tones until my father's spirits revived. My mother scorned their talk—"Men's talk," she called it, "tittle-tattle about the market." She looked knowingly at me when they went on like that together—and suddenly we were conspirators; the two men might be allies but so were we. In those moments I was her only true friend.

But my thoughts did not linger with my father very long—I did not even acknowledge the relief I felt that he was not accompanying us—for soon I was caught up in the excitement of the ferry that carried us across the Sound. There came a moment when neither shore was visible and we were conscious only of the firm beat of the engine, of wheeling gulls and distant bells. The other ferry came sliding by, our mirror image, passengers thronging the rails and children throwing Cracker Jacks to the clamoring birds. Both ships let loose mighty blasts. The universe trembled, and I leaned against my mother's skirt and reached for her hand, but she seemed far away—already she was on the road that would carry us north . . . and then the shore came into view, sun flashing off a distant car, a brick stack oozing dark smoke. We were moving swiftly alongside a breakwater whose heaped boulders were a creature risen from the sea. At the far end of the harbor two men lowered a gangplank. It fell toward us, a door unhinged.

My mother had an odd way of driving. She would place her foot down firmly on the accelerator and press it to the floor, the small Ford coupe springing forward like a pony stung by a bee. And then, as though she were astonished by the result, she would abruptly release it, the car gagging and sputtering, its dying momentum eliciting outraged responses from any vehicles that chanced to be following along behind us. "What is that awful man doing with his face up against my rear window!" she would exclaim; and as the indignant driver pulled out to pass, down her foot came again.

There was something zany and thrilling about it, and as we moved along through the depressed Connecticut mill towns I sat alertly beside her, bracing myself for the squeal of brakes and the agitated honking of horns. After Danbury her driving steadied a bit. She sat with her gloved hands high on the wheel and stared ahead as though she already knew how the maples stood by the sides of the fields, knew how all the houses and barns were arranged. We arrived at the first bridge and crossed over to the east bank of the Housatonic. Half a mile later we came to the covered bridge over the Belledame—*our* river, she called it—and as we rumbled across its planking I craned my head to see if through the slatted sides of the dark, dusty interior I could glimpse the rushing torrent below. Soon, proceeding beside its winding banks, climbing steadily through meadows and pine woods, we would come to the small towns I loved—Darlington, Hollenbeck, Grover, Mercersville, and finally our destination, Ellsworth Falls. But I knew these places mostly from the journey home, for now I began to fidget and yawn; and before long I would put my head on my mother's lap and stare sleepily up at her and through the open window at the branches high against the sky.

I was conscious of the pulse of her foot, of the pulse in her slender neck, of her marvelous husky voice beginning to weave its stories. Although they started gently—she would idle along about the look of the countryside in the days when horses drew carriages along the roads—these were not exactly lullabies; there was too much violence for that, and all the quiet talk about "olden days" was merely a prelude to stories of her amazing father. By the time she came to him her voice was like a croon. It had its pulse too, slipping in and out of the past like a crocheting needle through soft, comforting wool. And when she reached down to touch me, it was not to see if I was awake but only to confirm that I was still there, for she must have felt that even if I was dozing these tales would sink in. And softly she went on, the river at our side, the road turning and turning, the leaves making their tracings against the sky, her voice describing my grandfather and how once, long, long ago, he had lit up the world.

2

ALL THAT MARCH day a gusting wind blew lumps of wet snow against the store windows on Main Street. It shook the looping strands of rubber-insulated wire Clarence Starcliffe had strung through the elm trees. It made the early arrivals shiver on the hard wooden seats of their buckboards. Women and children sought shelter in the Ellsworth Inn; the men went off in another direction, into the saloons along Railroad Street.

My grandfather was oblivious of these things. Arriving at his laboratory at the break of dawn, he found once again that the Siemens generator failed to respond. He flung his jacket on the floor and set feverishly to work. By late morning, comforted by its steady hum, he went across the street to check—probably for the hundredth time—the induction coils he had laid out on the basement floor of the Sparks house. From there he followed his wires out onto the front lawn; and by late afternoon he was making his way slowly up Main Street, examining every inch of cable the way a sailor studies a hemp rope for hidden flaws. There were more people on the streets now, and the porches of the Inn, halfway down the block, were full of families huddling under their winter coats. The snow had stopped, but it was thundering in the distance and great fangs of lightning bit through the sky. "Someone up there knew I was about to trespass," he said later. "They weren't pleased."

On that blustering March day in 1886 the town of Ellsworth Falls looked much the way it does today. At the south end of Main there were a number of handsome clapboard houses set back under tall white pines. At the north end of the town, before the road turned off to the east and crossed the Belledame, there stood a pair of homely gray churches, one Catholic and one Protestant, eyeing each other like uneasy sentries across a disputed border. Between the houses and the churches stretched a single long block of red-brick stores, the lines of flat facades broken on one side by the beamy porches of the Inn and on the other by the brilliant red doors, slightly recessed, of the Ellsworth Fire Brigade, whose shiny gold-and-black hook and ladder stood at the ready that day, a little apart from the other wagons and buggies. Because the street was wide and the brick buildings low and rather plain, Ellsworth Falls—then as now—had more the appearance of a Western town than of a delicate New England village.

By nightfall, with wagons jammed into every inch of space, with men lurching out onto the street from the saloons, with children beginning to cry and mothers beginning to scold, the atmosphere was like that of a great country fair. It was remarkable so many people had come: farmers and millworkers from up and down the entire valley, doctors and teachers and librarians from the small neighboring towns, storekeepers from as far away as Orion—all of them had come, all stood with their cold breath smoking the air. Even the bearded loonies who lived in the hills brewing fierce spirits and awaiting Judgment Day had come. Perhaps Clarence Starcliffe would be the instrument of their redemption.

When, several weeks before, he had posted the notice that on March 16th, as soon after sunset as practicable, he would conduct his experiment, the curiosity of the entire county had been aroused. They still knew almost nothing about him, even though it was nearly five years since he had first appeared with his wife, Lila, and their infant son and set up his laboratory in the abandoned rubber factory along the river.

He was six foot five and weighed no more than a hundred and seventy pounds, and this made him either the tallest thin man or the thinnest tall man they had ever seen. He walked with a rapid, jerky stride, his head tilted slightly back, so he seemed always to be staring at the tops of buildings or at far-off hills. The women of the town saw him go by and put their hands up to their breasts for fear that, like a crane removed from its natural habitat, he would trip and fall. When they tried to draw him out, he replied only that he enjoyed "tinkering," and then darted away, as though the subject of his work were intimate to the point of shamefulness. But they knew that tinkerers did not sit in large workrooms like the ones in his laboratory; they did not surround themselves with elaborate festooned apparatus; and they did not labor with his kind of intensity. He seemed never to leave the place; he was there before dawn and long after nightfall, day after day, and now the days had stretched to months and years. Rumors abounded. He was at work on an incandescent "powder"; he was building a "dynamo." Schoolchildren crawled up close to the red-brick building and peered in with delicious tremblings. He was winding black thread, shiny as a coolie's hair, through a spiral winch. There were hummings and vibrations that could not be explained by the steady thrum of the river. Sudden bolts of light flew from one brass rod to another, and he flung up his hands—this man who hardly ever displayed emotion—and laughed uproariously. It was small wonder they thought him peculiar. The wonder was they never considered him dangerous.

As the day of his experiment drew near, his spirits flagged. Lila Starcliffe implored him not to lose heart. She was a tiny woman, and the sight of the two of them together would have been the source of mirth had it not been for her vigor and authoritativeness. Partly this was a matter of the set of her jaw, partly of the strength of her hands—they were large hands for a woman of her size, and she used them surely.

"Clarence, it will work!" she cried, trying to impart every bit of courage she possessed.

"Well, if it doesn't," he said ruefully, "we're done for. Look at this god-awful place."

They lived in a small cabin to the northeast of town. Except for a tiny flow of income from a few patents—a pair of carbon filaments, an air pump, a secondary battery—they had no source of support. He was a fine shot, she an extraordinary gardener. To an extent that would have astonished their neighbors, they lived off the land.

For years, before he had come up here, he had been a scientific nomad, moving from one laboratory to the next. He had a quick mind, he was a skilled draftsman. Why couldn't he do things the way he was told? Was he original or just plain ornery? He had this peculiar theory about electricity and how to send it over long distances. The trouble was, it stood all the other theories on their heads, and the men who employed him—some of them already famous—did not like to see their work thrown into question. He was never contentious; it was just that he couldn't seem to focus on anything but his own ideas. When he left one laboratory for another, the partings were amiable, more a matter of puzzlement than of anger or deep regret. It was said he was *odd*; it was hoped that someday soon he would settle down.

And so he had come to this quiet valley to try one more time, staking everything he possessed—his intellectual resources, the future of his family—on one last bold experiment. He would demonstrate the validity of his theory, not with drawings, not with equations, but by doing what no one else before had done—by lighting up an entire town.

"On that memorable night," my mother says, her voice a shade deeper, her excitement mounting, "the crowd grew impatient. The raucous men passed bottles from hand to hand.

When would he stop fussing? When would he get on with it? They were chilled through and through. Then they saw him coming slowly down the street. He went into Mr. Cobb's, the apothecary, to check the 150-candlepower lamp; into Mr. Norton's dry goods store—Mother and Father were *beholden* to the Nortons; they couldn't pay their bills, and still Mr. Norton accommodated them—and there he looked at the 60-candlepower lamps, different strengths for different stores, that was part of it. Do you think he noticed how little merchandise was left on display? Do you think he knew how scared they were, despite his gentle persuasions? They were all waiting now, rigid with cold and anticipation, the timid merchants, the families standing on the seats of the buckboards, the drunks. Hoots and catcalls came from the porch of the Inn."

Stationed at the south end of Main, Lila Starcliffe held Arthur close, trying to warm him. The boy stared up at Clarence Starcliffe with large brown eyes. "Will you lift me, Father?"

"Of course I will, son. In just a moment . . . a moment more."

He looked to the sky; his heart was pounding, his hand shook. He looked one more time down the long street, the buggies crammed together every which way. The crowd seemed immense, as though the whole county had gathered there—and now it was quiet, watching his every move. Clarence Starcliffe felt the wind on his face and smelled the sharp winter smells—coal fires and steaming manure from the stomping horses. He took a deep breath, as though he and the town and the world might never be the same again.

It seemed like a single fluid motion, the way he leaned forward, pushed down hard on the metal lever, and then practically flung Arthur up onto his shoulders. The crowd was still hushed. No one could take his eyes from the wires. It was as though the mysterious essence flowing there would emit a strange odor or "convulse," my mother says, "like a snake shedding its skin." But there was no smell, no sound, not even a tremor. Nothing happened—for an eternity of time, nothing! And perhaps that would have been a wonderful thing, with no danger in it, a marvelous joke—and a vindication, for hadn't they known all along that he was queer in the head? You could feel the laughter building.

But then—then it *came*, the ghostly, flickering light.

As he walked down the street, his son astride his shoulders, the light gathered strength and flung itself boldly from the storefronts and lay on the dark, damp streets like slabs of butter. The crowd gave a sigh. Hesitantly a few people moved forward, then a few more; then they moved in a headlong rush and pressed against the windows and stared in at the bare bulbs with their trembling orange filaments. They had no interest in the objects illuminated, only in the light, as though it were alive and if they drew close enough they could feel its warmth, touch it, and be lit up themselves.

3

AT FIRST THERE WAS only the story in the Orion *Sentinel*; a week later, another in the Hollenbeck *Courier*. But as the lights kept burning—the townspeople refused to let Clarence Starcliffe turn them off—the word spread far and wide. Reporters came to Ellsworth Falls; then they began tracking down the inventors whose theories had been refuted.

Oh yes, one of the great men said—he was standing in Herald Square in New York City, and the journalists hung on his every word—he knew about Mr. Starcliffe and his alternating currents, he knew about his induction coils and his converters. Mr. Starcliffe had worked for him once in his laboratory over in New Jersey. He took his cap off and did a little jig, crying, "Why, he cannot make it *safe*, he cannot make it re-*lie*-able, he cannot make it sell by meter!" He jumped in the air, as if he were shouting "Hooray!" The New York *World* printed his words as a jingle. The *Sentinel* picked it up and ran it under a cartoon: Clarence Starcliffe's oblong face a bulb, his eyes a pair of filaments, his hair standing on end. At first you thought he was a country boy who had been "had"; but when you studied the expression on the face of the bulb, you weren't entirely sure.

The joviality of the great men vanished when the results of the experiment finally sank in. The distance the current had been conveyed, the steadiness of the current, the characteristics of the wire—these facts could not be denied; they made it clear that when the towns and cities of the land were lit up, it would be done Clarence Starcliffe's way, not theirs. They met in secret conclave in Pittsburgh, where one of them had a laboratory and a small factory designed to produce the first trial runs of electrical equipment. It was evident to them that this was equipment for which there would no longer be much demand. They agreed they would not stand idly by.

If Clarence Starcliffe expected to return to the peace of his laboratory, he was mistaken. If he expected other kinds of peace, he was mistaken again. The world came to him for illumination—it came to him for Starcliffe alternating-current motors and transformers and dynamo electric machines. It came to him as not many years before prospectors, with their motley hangers-on, had come swarming to the Western mining fields. He was besieged by municipal officials wishing to place orders, by bankers wishing to provide capital, by fly-by-night lawyers wishing to help him license, incorporate, export, borrow, and if necessary, steal, in order to feather his own and their nests. Thus was the Starcliffe Works born, a graceful, narrow-windowed brick factory on the Belledame, not far above town. Thus Clarence Starcliffe, tinkerer, became Clarence Starcliffe, manufacturer. Thus began the endless patent suits with the inventors in whose laboratories he had done his early work and who claimed now the inventions belonged to them. Thus his troubles began.

For solace he built himself an eccentric house on the banks of the river, south of town. It was there his second son, Frederick, known as Flint, and his daughter, Sarah, were born in the last decade of the century.

And now my mother's voice is describing my grandfather's house, massive, shingled, Victorian, and yet airy as a summer pavilion. Its curved verandas were decorated with Japanese latticework and keyhole arches, its windows adorned with scalloped fringes and filigreed balconies. These things gave the place a beribboned and festive air, almost like a Mississippi paddle-wheeler. Up high the mansard roof was framed by a pair of slender brick chimneys. Under the eaves was a row of small carved figures, gentle angels and cherubs smiling down from their shelter, their wood rosy in the late afternoon sun. Often my mother imagined she was up there with them and saw the world through their eyes, the French gardens smelling of rose and apricot and thyme, the cool green river moving along slowly between low banks. Beyond the river, fields stretched away, sometimes planted in corn, sometimes lying fallow. And far off to the west were low hills that climbed in gentle steps to the rounded summit called the Dome. On clear days she and her father rode on their horses across the fields, all the way to the top. It was the highest peak in this part of the country, and from it one could look over the valley, over the river, over this very house. From that vantage point its chimneys were like minarets, its convoluted facade like a temple's in a far-off land. It was not hard to imagine priests moving slowly through the gardens, animals come from the forest to drink at fountains, and through the violet mist rising from the river the faint shimmering of gongs.

4

WHEN I CLIMB TO the Dome now, eighty years after my grandfather built his splendid home, all that can be seen of it, all that is left, are the two chimneys rising from a green forest.

I scan the river valley, looking for my own house, always feeling a tremor of apprehension. There it is—I feel the relief—six miles downstream from those austere, mocking chimneys, a small brick structure. The apple trees, the cryptomeria, the cedars—I have planted them myself—frame it pleasantly, the river falling away to the south. I have left my daughter there riding high over the water on a wooden swing. I cannot see her from this distance but imagine her with her long tanned legs out straight, her arms gripping the ropes, her face tilting up toward the boundless sky.

In each of us there lies a hidden fragment of the past—a place, a moment, a figure—that is like a touchstone, that object used from time immemorial to test the authenticity of precious metals. We rub our lives against such a stone—often hardly aware we are doing so—the way a cat rubs its back against the leg of a chair. In my youth, my mother's voice was such a touchstone, and it was as though she were bequeathing her past to me before I was old enough to have one of my own.

Now it is more than thirty years since I lay with my head in her lap, the car ebbing and flowing along the banks of the Belledame. Now I know the stories better than she—the tales of how her father lit up the streets of Ellsworth Falls and how my other grandfather—foolish, valiant man!—struggled to wrest marble from the earth, and of how my parents first met and journeyed out into the world together. When, later, I discovered that my touchstone was not trustworthy, I wanted to cry out to my mother, "No, it was not that way, what you told me was not true!" But by then it was too late; there was no one, really, to cry out to.

Will my daughter feel the same way when she ponders this story, which by then will have become *hers*? Will she understand that as we uncover one mystery, another comes to take its place? Will she understand that voices are not what they seem, nor mirrors that we hold to our faces, nor even that pair of chimneys across the valley cloaked in green?

5

WHEN MY UNCLE ARTHUR graduated from Yale he went to work for a bank in Hartford, the idea being that after he had learned all there was to know about money he would return to Ellsworth Falls to help with the running of the Starcliffe Works. In the winter of 1909 my grandfather had a heart attack, and Arthur was summoned, far sooner than anyone had expected.

Until then he had seen only the fruits of his father's ingenuity: the elaborate Victorian mansion on the river, the stables full of Morgans and Appaloosa and Tennessee walking horses, the carriage houses with their gleaming buckboards and cabriolets. There was a Saint-Gaudens frieze in one of the formal gardens, a Delacroix hunting scene—two horsemen in ardent pursuit of a spotted leopard—on one of the living room walls, a series of exquisite Piranesi etchings in Clarence Starcliffe's study. Half a dozen men tended the grounds, stocked the ponds and streams, cared for the animals. Indoors there were parlor and scullery maids and a cook. The burgeoning staff made Lila Starcliffe fretful; she distrusted them; she knew she could do their tasks—from shoeing a horse to marinating a lamb—far better than they. She could never free herself from the thought that God's largesse (she saw it in those terms) would not last, that someday she would be called upon to do these things again. When Arthur went up to the Works and started to study the accounts, he began to share her uneasiness.

His father had not paid attention to the factory for years. Apparently he believed he had invented a kind of perpetual money machine, the profits from which could be poured indefinitely into the fashioning of his paradise along the banks of the river. The accounting records were chaotic; the lawsuits from the old inventors still festered—demands for back royalties amounted, incredibly, to more than a million dollars. The documentation necessary to fight the suits—employment contracts, patent applications, letters—was scattered in law offices and courthouses from Orion to Washington, D.C. And to make matters worse, the business was no longer as prosperous as before: there were competitors with newer plants and more advanced designs.

Arthur set to work like a man in a fury. He was only

twenty-seven years old, diminutive, delicate-featured, with the same kind of prickly determination as his mother. He grew a mustache, hoping it would lend him an air of authority. And perhaps it did, for it was stiff and prim and, before long, flecked with white. But it wasn't really necessary: the glow in his brown eyes, the set of his jaw—these were authority enough. He dug into things. He took nothing for granted, especially the easy answers given by the aging, complacent men who served as surrogates for his father and were interested, he quickly concluded, only in preserving the pattern of their days. After a bitter argument, a number of workers were let go.

For nearly twenty years orders had poured into the Starcliffe Works from all over the world. For nearly twenty years this had been the only place in the valley where you could be sure of your job and where there were even likely to be a few new ones each summer for the boys getting out of school. But now, instead of employing three hundred workers, the plant employed only two hundred and fifty. Suddenly there was resentment in people's faces; when Arthur walked through the production lines, the men turned away.

A delegation came to pay a call on Clarence Starcliffe. He sat, old and frail, in a high-backed wicker chair on one of his verandas. Before his illness he had grown accustomed to traveling abroad to give papers before scientific societies. He had made those journeys over two decades, each trip further whetting his appetite for paintings and sculptures and fine antique furniture. He had become an avid collector, and now he sat in his chair and studied dealers' catalogues, making notes. Sometimes he scratched out an equation or made a quick drawing—tiny spools, and coils of wire as delicate as flowers.

There were three of them. Sitting in another high-backed chair in a far corner of the porch, my mother, a sketch pad in her lap, watched them walk slowly across the lawn; they reminded her of the farmers, hair slicked back, all agog, who came into town each August for the Ellsworth Fair. They paused before one of the marble statues, a naked boy with an arrow. Coming closer, they craned their heads at the immense facade of the house, and when at last they stood before Clarence Starcliffe, they were like subjects before a king—shy, clumsy, adoring—or so my mother thought. She was just thirteen years old, too old now to crawl up in her father's lap, too young to know anything of the cares of the world. The men did not notice her sitting there; they did not see the expression that crossed her face when instead of paying obeisance they began to spill out their grievances, their voices rising, the oldest of the three shouting something about "the boy . . . the boy doesn't understand, Clarence!" and then her father was pulling himself up out of his chair and stood towering above them. They stepped back and stared at him as they had previously examined the front of the house. She thought he would order them from the grounds. But no, he was only moved, he was *sorry*; he held one of them by the arm and spoke softly of the old days when there had always been a job for someone in need. They saw his bewilderment; they sensed his pain, only theirs was worse.

For years it had been a matter of both amusement and incredulity in Orion County that this house, of all houses, had never been wired for electricity. People took it as another sign of Clarence Starcliffe's eccentricity, but he and Lila Starcliffe simply preferred the older light. They liked to eat with candles on the dining-room table; they liked to read by kerosene lamp—the glow was softer, it was warmer, it cast different kinds of shadows. Now, not knowing what to do, he looked at the men and offered to give half a dozen of them the task of wiring up the place. They shook his hand and went sullenly down the steps, their interest in the sumptuous grounds lost in a swell of bitterness. They understood his gesture was well-meant, and they accepted it. But they saw it as only that: a gesture. They saw too, from his frailty, that there was nothing he could do about the new state of affairs at the Works. The boy would remain in command.

Arthur was furious about the offer. "Good God, Father," he exclaimed, "what good does it do if I put a little money in one of our pockets if you go and take it out the other?"

My mother had never heard Arthur address him this way before. She could not bear her father's abject look and she fled from the room, seeking Flint. As usual he was on the front lawn, practicing approach shots, the white balls arching prettily under the high elms and landing near a blanket he had placed on the grass twenty or so yards away. He didn't seem the least bit upset by what she said. He told her not to worry, their father would put his foot down if Arthur went too far.

"Oh, Flint, he won't. He's *old*. Can't you see?"

Always Lila Starcliffe tried to weave a cocoon of calm around her husband. The evening meal was an important part of it, a time of quiet and replenishment for all of them, the family sitting together enjoying the bounty of the land—speckled trout from the river, partridge and woodcock from the hills, vegetables and fruit from the gardens. If Arthur tried to bring up business matters, his mother gave him a sharp look or reached out a hand and ended it. But on this particular evening she had no chance to stop my mother from blurting, "Arthur, why did you fire those men? They need the work, don't they?"

His cheeks were still a little flushed from his earlier encounter. He put his napkin down and tried to compose himself.

"Of course they do. I didn't *want* to do it—surely you know that?"

"I don't know a thing. No one ever explains—"

"Sarah," said Lila Starcliffe, "that will do."

Silence returned. Lila Starcliffe went out into the pantry and came back. Flint sat quietly with the same dreamy expression as his father's, but if any equations danced in his head they had to do with the parabolic flight of golf balls—Flint was studying golf at Yale, or so it seemed. Arthur barely touched his food; his hands played nervously with the silver and his darting eyes returned again and again to his father's face. Clarence Starcliffe stared at the flames of the candles.

Almost feverish now, Arthur suddenly stopped twisting in his seat; he took an unexpected, deep, shuddering breath. And at last, after that uneasy silence, he began to talk in a solemn voice, pouring out his fears about the condition of the Works, about the need to dismiss more men, of the need, especially, to settle the old suits. He had been worrying about these things ever since his return, but he had kept them to himself. He had never before betrayed his anguish or his fear.

"Arthur," Lila Starcliffe said, and then, imploringly, "Oh, Arthur, please."

But he would not be silenced—not on that night or on the nights to come over the rest of the summer and into the fall. My mother felt she was the one who had started him off. He could tolerate the resentment of the men at the plant; he could bear the scorn of the town; but if his sister—if his very own family—was harboring doubts about him, then he would speak out, he would explain the situation, even if it meant disturbing his father's precious silence, even if it meant incurring his mother's wrath. It was not the explanations as such that my mother minded; it was the bitterness in his voice.

And when, months later, they still did not seem to understand, he cried out again, "Don't any of you *see*—don't you see what's at stake?" He flung his arms out over the snowy tablecloth, embracing not just the candelabra and the silverware but the whole vast house, the lawns, the gardens, the stables, the fields stretching to the distant hills. "All of this," he said, and my mother felt a shiver go down her spine. "Oh,

Father," he said, "it happened so long ago. I don't know the facts. Please *help* me, Father—help me gather the papers, help me settle the claims."

Startled, Clarence Starcliffe looked up.

"Father, please."

Reluctantly, he agreed.

So the documents came—in bulky manila envelopes, in suitcases and old steamer trunks—and in the evenings Clarence Starcliffe went into his study, taking my mother with him to help sort things out. He was secretly pleased; it was like discovering old friends. And he saw that much of it would come in handy for the paper he was expecting to give that spring—not a paper for London or Heidelberg or Rome, but for Ellsworth Falls. The town was planning a celebration of the twenty-fifth anniversary of his experiment—a quarter of a century, think of it, Sarah!—and he sat studying his old journals, savoring the details, long forgotten, of that momentous event. He was most grateful to Arthur. He understood the boy's impatience—of course he was wild to get his hands on these things. But first he must refresh his memory, prepare his talk. Then Arthur and the lawyers could work their will—settle with the scoundrels if they must.

When he delivered his paper, his hands trembled on the edge of the lectern and his voice was unsteady. The whole room was straining to hear, hundreds of people, every chair in the Sparks ballroom taken. My mother longed to cry out that he was not like other men. His hands and voice might tremble, but when he looked to the green hills he did not see them as others did. His eyes pierced the surface of things and under the surface light quivered and darted and sprang, and only he was able to hold it and make it rest.

"It was a beautiful speech, Father," said Flint as they drove home in one of the carriages.

"Think they understood a word of it?"

"Since when," said Lila Starcliffe, "has anyone *understood* you, Clarence?"

"As we drove up the avenue of beeches," my mother tells me, "there was a wonderful dancing light in the windows of the house. You could see it through the lattices, through the arches. It was like a child's scribbling, jagged orange crayon marks against the shingled walls. Over the roof there hung a bladder of smoke, an evil thing, as though on this marvelous starry night a single cloud had come from over the horizon to hover there. It was such a glorious night! I remember leaning forward to put my arms around Father's shoulders and rest my head against his. But I could not take my eyes off that cloud; it was eddying into the pines, it oozed and roiled into the eaves, shrouding the heads of my dear cherubs.

" 'My God,' said Arthur, 'it's on fire!'

" 'It's not—' I cried, 'it can't be!'

" 'Go back, boy,' said Father. 'Go for the hook and ladder!'

"Arthur turned the carriage; the horses reared and made a fearful clatter. The rest of us raced across the lawn, Father walking along slowly behind us. He tried to mount the steps, but the heat from the porch forced him back. Mother clung to Flint. It was as though the flames had swept across her face and left it bare. Flames climbed the front of the house, feeding on the luscious shingles. By the time Arthur returned, by the time the hook and ladder came clanging over the bridge, it was too late. Oh, Peter, the house was gone!"

6

FOR WANT OF proper safekeeping her father's papers were lost. For want of the papers the patent suits were lost and her father forced to pay his former colleagues substantial royalties on the sales of Starcliffe electrical equipment. For want of adequate funds to make these payments, the Starcliffe Works hovered on the edge of bankruptcy. To my mother the events unfolded like a somber fairy tale, all the elements ordained, each step leading to the next.

The family moved to an ugly gray house on one of the poor back streets in town. It was a cramped place with low ceilings. A rocky hillside rose sharply in the back, cutting off sunlight by midafternoon.

Had the fire been set? Was it true—as the rumors said—that a small band of the laid-off men had lit a match to the place? How else account for its breaking out on a night when everyone—family and servants—had gone into town for the celebration? These stories added to Arthur's burdens. He no longer spoke at the dinner table; he kept his troubles—and theirs—to himself.

In contrast, Clarence Starcliffe was full of bravado. He had returned to his laboratory. He leaned back in his chair and told them of the new theories and inventions hatching in his head. When their fortunes were restored, he would rebuild their rural paradise, and their intended lives would resume. Lila Starcliffe could not bear to look at him when he spoke this way. My mother threw him tender glances; encouraged, he smiled back at her and went on.

But when my mother went to the laboratory in the late afternoons she would find him staring out the window with a lost expression, the room littered with papers and old equipment. One autumn day he had his head down on his desk. She touched him gently, "Father, it's time to go home."

He groaned and raised himself a little. "Fetch Doctor Willoughby, child. I'm ill."

They took him to the hospital, and a week later he was dead.

At the funeral Lila Starcliffe stood with quiet dignity on the steps of the church and shook hands with friends and neighbors, fixing with her baleful stare only that small group of famous men, the old inventors who had come sheepishly to pay their respects. Clarence Starcliffe had said of her that she had an Old and a New Testament side—she could be stern and loving, she could lay down the law and forgive, but God help you if you crossed her when she wasn't in one of her forgiving moods.

Little by little in the dark house her voice grew sharper, her judgments more severe. She dressed only in black. She no longer went into town. Did she believe the stories about the fire being set? Or was her memory harkening back to an earlier time when the town had laughed at Clarence? Either way she held herself aloof, a proud woman unwilling to acknowledge defeat.

When the country entered the war, Flint joined the army, and Arthur took advantage of improved business prospects to sell the Works. He settled the back royalty claims. Armed with letters of recommendation from the men with whom he had done business—those older men, suppliers and creditors, who had been impressed with his diligence and courage—he went to New York in search of a job and found one with Grenfell and Company, the finest banking firm of that day. It was there that his famous career began.

Alone, her school days finished, my mother tried at first to break free. She spoke to Arthur about finding a job, but he would have none of it—her place was here, looking after their mother. One day when she announced to her mother that she had been offered a position as sales clerk in Cobb's Pharmacy, Lila Starcliffe responded, "We are not tradespeople, Sarah."

She had been cut off from the world before, in the house along the river. But that had been a happy land, an abundant garden, and always her father had been at the center of it. She had had no need of school friends then; she had needed only to be with him, the two of them sitting in their high-backed wicker chairs, Clarence Starcliffe in his white suit glowing like a filament in one of his slender bulbs. Now she and her mother went stoically about their household chores; they knitted sweaters for the men at the front; they corresponded with Flint.

At Yale, Flint had discovered golf; in the army, cards. He wrote them from France, telling them nothing of mud and mortar shells, only of royal flushes and grand slams.

7

I MYSELF KNOW that dark gray house where my mother and grandmother lived alone during the First World War. It was to this house that we drove on the eve of the next war. When we arrived, we would find my grandmother sitting alone in the low-ceilinged living room, a tiny white-haired woman with blazing eyes. I would lean over to kiss her cheek; she did not smile. She was almost stone-deaf by then, and her stillness frightened me. And yet there was something else about her that gripped me.

I was conscious of her slipping into my room in the early hours of the morning and pulling the blankets up snugly around my shoulder, her palm resting for a moment on my forehead. Once or twice when she thought the house was empty, I found her standing in the kitchen door, staring out, singing a tune, her voice rough from disuse and badly off-key. She did not know I was behind her; she could not hear me or her tune, and I moved away, not wishing to disturb her privacy. In the evenings when we played double solitaire, she reached out a hand, her fingers cool as bone, and showed me which card to turn. In these small ways, I came to share her silence, and it was not so frightening after all. In my own home there were more frightening things.

When it came time to go, my mother sat at the breakfast table, sipping her coffee, lingering, and for once I was not impatient for us to be off. It was hard to leave the old woman. Were we sorry for her? Or sorry for ourselves? The cocoon of calm she had once wished to weave around her husband she had now woven around herself; or it had been woven for her, the threads dense and strong as wire mesh.

In the car again, we moved slowly down the road, and for a long time I sat on my knees in the front seat, looking back. The pull was strong, and soon we would return.

8

"GOOD GOD," said Flint when he returned from the war, "have you been here all this time? It's like some kind of *nunnery*." He stood on the street in his corporal's uniform and stared first at the house and then at his pretty sister; she was a dark-haired beauty. "We must do something, Sarah," he said. "You're twenty-one years old. Time you got away! Time you had a beau!"

"Why," she said, "I'm sure I'd be most happy to oblige. Who, exactly, is the lucky man to be?"

Flint rented a farmhouse down the valley in Mercersville. At first my mother thought he'd done it for her—as a way of getting her out of Ellsworth Falls. But soon it was clear he needed to escape too, not from Ellsworth Falls, but from New York.

Arthur had found him a job in a brokerage house. Arthur, beginning to make a name for himself, was anxious for Flint's success too; he was always looking over his shoulder, exhorting him on. And so on weekends Flint fled to the hills. On Saturday nights his farmhouse rocked with music and laughter. His kitchen became a small gambling den, and for a few small hours each weekend he was in his element.

A stranger walking down the dirt road by Flint's house on a summer night would have encountered the delicious aroma of lamb roasting on a spit; he would have heard the gentle chunking of horseshoes against sand, several of the men moving slowly about, playing on into the darkness. From the parlor, where couples were gathered around an upright piano, came the mellow notes of an Irish air. Perhaps he would have seen my mother helping Flint with the dinner, carrying plates from the kitchen out onto the lawn, or standing for a moment on the porch and looking over the quiet countryside, the hay almost ready for cutting, fireflies flitting about, frogs gallumphing in the wet places along the sides of the meadow.

It was on just such an evening, my mother standing on the porch in just such a way, the first couples beginning to arrive, that a young man she had never seen before came striding toward her in a dark-blue suit and shoes as orange as tortoise shells.

"I'm Henry Kempton," he said, sticking out his hand. He was all polished and bright; there was a newness not only to his suit but to his pink cheeks and his blue eyes, so large and eager they seemed newly hatched. "I've come to the right place? You *are* Flint's sister?"

He still held her hand; shyly, she drew it back. "Oh, yes. Sister and slave."

"We met on the train," he said with a gust of laughter. "He roped me into a game of bridge. Wiped me out too!"

Flint had not said a word about him. When the young man saw this, his confidence ebbed. He ran a hand through his close-cropped sandy hair and stood there forlornly like someone reporting for work on the wrong day. She felt her breath let go, surprised she had been holding it in so.

He had a lovely tenor voice; soon he was standing with the others harmonizing at the piano. He didn't know how to play poker, but wanted to learn; he was at the table at Flint's side. The pile of chips before him dwindled. He kept reaching into his pocket for more change. He didn't seem to mind; he kept laughing; his rough laughter filled the kitchen and floated out onto the porch where she stood wondering why his eagerness and vulnerability moved her so.

The next Saturday he was back, this time with his sister Agatha. The two of them worked in the city, Henry in a Wall Street firm and Agatha in a department store, and on weekends they came to stay with their parents in a house down the road. Aggie wore a loud dress that lit up the men's eyes. She had red hair and pale skin and an easy way. Late in the evening she stood next to my mother, smoking a cigarette. "Guess what I'm doing this Monday night, dearie?"

My mother couldn't imagine.

"I'm going out with my boss—it's the first time. Ira must be fifty. Henry is such a shy sweetie; he won't come out and say so—he just coughs his way around it—but he disapproves. He thinks I might have to *put out*." She winked at my mother and tugged her dress up over her ample bosom.

"But what will you *talk* about?"

"About lingerie, precious! That's my department. I do the buying. Ira still keeps his hand in, of course."

When Henry and Agatha talked together they were more than brother and sister, they were comrades in arms. It appeared then as though the worlds of stocks and bonds and lingerie were the same. My mother was surprised, for Arthur always made his business affairs solemn and mysterious. Was this just his way, or did it have something to do with her? Why did she find it so hard to respond when Henry began telling her about his firm and the clever Englishman who ran it? It was clear he adored him, clear that he reveled in their ingenious undertakings; but soon she could feel her interest slackening and it must have shown, for he would begin to labor with her like a teacher with a slow child.

The day he asked her to go on a picnic, she felt a stab of panic—what would they say and do when they were alone? He had a special place to show her, he said, he had a story to tell her. She missed the urgency in his voice; she did not see the troubled look in his eyes.

She could hardly keep up with him on the steep wooded path, and when they came out into the meadow at the top she was out of breath.

"There," he said. At first she thought he meant the Dome, shimmering off in the distance across the valley. "No—over there!"

At the far end of the meadow, in the shade of the woods, she made out dim forms: a tin shack covered with trumpet vine, wooden scaffolding, a block of stone. Then she saw a whole row of squared-off blocks; deeper in the woods, still more of them, piled into steps, as though someone had started to build a pyramid on the top of the hill and thought better of it.

"My father's folly," he cried, hurling his rough laughter at the boulders.

He took her by the hand and led her across the meadow until they stood at the edge of a rectangular pit; a sour odor came up from the bottom. In the darkness of the woods she saw an old derrick hung with tattered ropes and rusty chains.

"It's a quarry. My father's marble quarry."

"It doesn't look like marble."

"No, it's a special kind. Father wanted to sell it for post offices."

She studied the stone more closely, saw the tiny bluish capillaries running through it. "But did anyone *want* it?"

"No," he said bitterly, putting down their things. "No one has ever wanted it, and I vouch no one ever will."

9

HE WAS TWELVE years old that first summer they went to visit his Uncle Oliver in Mercersville. He would never forget the trip, the suitcases piled in their dark front hall, the mad dash to the Back Bay station, the train sliding along past dull factories and out into the flat countryside. Time and space opened in a marvelous unbounded vista—the beginning of a country summer, in the summer of his youth.

His father was all dressed up in a new seersucker suit and a boater with a bright green band. He was a slight man, pale and a little bent from working long hours in the small print shop he owned on the outskirts of Boston. When he came home in the evenings his fingers gave off a dry inky smell. He spent much time dreaming of greater things, especially of owning his own newspaper, of being a newspaperman who could actually create stories, not simply mechanically transmute them from one form to another. That was what he pretended to be as he rambled up and down the aisles, approaching other passengers and with guileless ardor asking them all kinds of questions; he was a reporter gathering stories, like a fisherman on an excursion with a net and a line.

He came back from these forays with tales of lust and violence and of the accumulation of amazing fortunes (these last were the ones he liked best). Emma Kempton, a plump, beaming woman encumbered with cloth valises and balls of yarn, found these sagas as satisfying as Boston cream pie. Agatha would interrupt cheerfully, "Oh, Poppa, you're making it all up." And Henry was all eyes.

At Orion they boarded a trolley for the trip down the valley. The occasional mansion they saw on the far side of the river was invested with the magic of Millard Kempton's stories. He could see himself living in one of these establishments in a kind of perennial ecstasy of success. Henry felt his excitement mounting, but for another reason: soon he would see Uncle Oliver, whom he adored. He told even better tales than his father; his had actually happened to him, his were *real*.

He stood at the trolley stop, a corpulent, broad-shouldered man fanning himself with a Panama hat. Henry ran, jumped into his arms, and scissored his small legs around his fleshy girth.

"Hey, sonny, grown a foot I bet."

Oliver was an engineer and a soldier of fortune. The boy associated the word "engineer" with railroads and soaring bridges. And "soldier of fortune"? His uncle had fought with Teddy Roosevelt; he had been wounded in the battle of San Juan Hill and had a puckered scar along the side of his rib cage to show for it. Now he was retired and lived in a simple country house with a low porch in front, a covered passageway leading to an immense barn out in back. There were fields to the right and left and a steep wooded hill behind the house that led to wilder meadows, full of flowers, higher up. It was in these woods a week later that Millard Kempton made his discovery. He came rushing down the path, a tear in one of his trouser legs and his sparse hair flying, and found Oliver and Henry in the cool barn hammering boards for the construction of a fort.

"Millard," cried Oliver, "what's happened? Look at you!"

"Took a header up there." He was gasping; the gleam was in his eye. "Fell flat on my face. But Ollie, look at these!" He held out a handful of mottled blue stones. "I reached out for something, to stop me from rolling down the hill, and came up with them."

Oliver rolled several of the stones between his fingertips and held them up to his great florid face like a jeweler studying gems. "Take a look, sonny," he said at last. "On the path, Millard? Are there more?"

"The whole hillside is covered with them!" He spoke with the wonder of a woman who sees that the floor of a forest has burst into fragrant bloom.

"Lordy."

Soon the two men and the boy were up in the woods, bending over the path, gathering the small, shiny pieces of rock.

The man they needed to talk to, said Oliver Kempton, was Skeeles—Frank "Jumbo" Skeeles. Gold, iron, oil, copper, timber—Jumbo Skeeles knew them all. Oliver had met him in Bogotá. A born wildcatter. Heart of a lion. "The stories I could tell you!"

Millard and Oliver and Henry took the trolley to Ellsworth Falls and met Skeeles in a saloon. Millard carried a leather satchel filled with stones. They sat in a booth, the three men drinking whisky, and Skeeles—a scrawny creature with a hooked nose and exceedingly sharp eyes—fondled the rocks in the dull light. "Only ten miles from here, you say? Lying alongside the path? *On the surface?*"

He accompanied them to Mercersville and climbed the wooded path—up "the mountain," as they began to call it. When they came out into the meadow he started across it like a hound on a scent, zigzagging this way and that. Henry ran along behind, trying to keep up. Skeeles stopped; his nose dipped; he moved on, stopped again, reached down and scrabbled the earth. Then he threw his head back.

"Here!" he roared. The word made the air shiver. "Here, here, here, here . . ." The whole valley seemed to listen and the clouds stop in their stately paths. "We should go in here, at the top."

"But how will we get the marble out to the road?" asked Millard.

"We'll build a railroad," said the engineer. "Single gauge."

"And that," my father told my mother, "is how our nightmare began."

His rough laughter had an edge, his face a dark quality as thick as earth. My mother looked across the meadow where they sat; it was bright with Queen Anne's lace; against the woods were lurid clumps of loosestrife. The day had a lofty August sky and all about them were the soft warm hummings of insects and feeding bees. She looked again at the squares of marble and wondered how they could possibly be a source of so much pain. She wondered if he wasn't exaggerating a little, for up to now he had shown no troubled side; she thought him the least mournful man she had ever met. As he continued, telling her of their wild hopes, of the quarries springing up across the land, of the marble courthouses and bank buildings—"all those marble columns and marble steps!"—she longed to soften his distress; she was sure she could. "But how wonderfully romantic," she cried, "to have dreams like that."

"Oh, no, you don't understand."

And he told her more.

He and his father went out to raise "a little capital," as Oliver put it. He hated the way his father stood in the dimly lit hallways of the Boston apartment houses and practiced his winning smile; he hated standing behind him, his heart beating clumsily, his palms moist, the heavy satchel parked between his legs.

The people who answered the doorbells were usually old; often they were in their bathrobes and slippers. Before long the two of them were sitting in overfurnished parlors much like their own, the smell of pot roast lingering in the air, his father bringing out the handsome prospectus—printed on his own press—for the Kempton Marble Company. There came a hushed moment when he was instructed to open the satchel and spread out the stones. "There now," Millard Kempton exclaimed, "aren't they beauts!" But the faces of the gentle old people always twisted a little and fell.

Sooner or later they reached for their pocketbooks. It was more like giving money to a missionary society than to a pair of con men—how could these two possibly mean any harm? And in it came, sometimes ten dollars, sometimes twenty-five or even fifty or a hundred. In the late evenings Emma Kempton would greet them, proud of "her boys" and their "take." Agatha, the bookkeeper, entered the amounts in a gray-and-red ledger and prepared the stock certificates for mailing. By the next summer they had raised nearly fifteen thousand dollars. It seemed to go in a flash. Skeeles bought a derrick and pumps and drills. In the barn out in back of Oliver's house, burlap bags bulged with sticks of dynamite. The blasting rent the peaceful air of the valley; it raised huge clouds of dust; it made the sheep in neighboring fields cringe against the low stone walls.

They ran out of money, of course, and raised more, ranging far and wide across the state, bringing with them photographs that showed the blocks of marble standing in the meadow like monuments from an archaeological excavation.

Into the air of this meadow my father shouted, "They were like vainglorious English generals hatching a geological Verdun!" My mother studied the marble again. From the earth came overarching trees and vines that shaded and gripped the blocks; it was not hard to imagine them being pulled back into the soil again, covered, forgotten.

The years went by, and because of Millard Kempton's folly the family fortunes were altered. Instead of attending Smith, Agatha found a job in a clothing store on Washington Street. As it turned out, she loved it, and the store loved her, and before long she had a better offer from a larger establishment in New York. Henry wanted to find a job too, but his father said he was to go to Yale; it was one of his many dreams. And so Henry went to New Haven on a scholarship, working in laundries and kitchens and selling tiepins and cuff links to his classmates, door to door.

"I was good at it," he said. "I could be charming and ingratiating and"—spitting out the word—"*unctuous*. I had learned by watching my father beg."

When the war came he enlisted in the army, pleading with his father to declare bankruptcy and bring the fiasco to an end. Their troubles were multiplying. Skeeles had run off, taking much of the equipment. Angry letters were coming in from investors demanding to know when the first marble would be sold, when the first dividends would be paid. And still Oliver's railroad had not been built.

But Millard Kempton would not listen. He was a mild man who had been stirred by the discovery of his own courage. He explained that he was making arrangements to sell his print shop. He and Emma Kempton would move to Mercersville and, with the capital raised from the sale of his business, they would keep the quarrry going. "It's only the war that's scared people," he said, "they've lost their nerve."

Millard Kempton wrote him long letters still full of dreams. My father would read them and rip them to shreds. Once, billeted in an old farmhouse in Brittany, he flung the tatters out the window and watched them float, vagrant blossoms, into the blossoming orchard below. It was Agatha who wrote him the news of their insolvency and of the agreement that had been reached to pay off the shareholders. They would get only ten cents on the dollar, but still, by now, the amount was not insubstantial. She was helping out a little each week. When he came home, he would have to help too.

"And have you?" my mother asked.

He did not answer. He looked at the grass, his face closed in with regret. She waited, and still he did not reply. It was as though he were ashamed—ashamed to tell her if he had, for then he would seem as foolish as his father before him; ashamed if he had not, for that would make him heartless.

"Anyway," she said, taking his hand and holding it in her lap and smiling at him, "it's over now—over and done with."

10

WHEN MY MOTHER tells the stories about my father, we are usually on our way home from Ellsworth Falls. This has something to do with her manner of telling, for now we are driving toward my father, not my grandmother; instead of lowering her voice so it is as dark as an ancient bard's, she is brisk and even a little sardonic. She likes to encapsulate the story of the marble quarry in little bubbles of humor. The participants are "characters"; they are "comical," which is to say that the whole affair is a little absurd—my father too, for taking it so seriously. It is very different from the way she tells the Starcliffe tales—as though the Kemptons only tinkered with life, while her father helped invent it.

She describes Clarence Starcliffe sitting in a wicker chair "glowing like a filament." Of course he was brilliant. Of course Millard Kempton was foolish. But in her renderings there is an element of caricature in both, grandiloquence being no less stilted than sentiment. By trying to make one larger and the other smaller than life, she doesn't get either of them quite right.

And my mother and father in these stories? How do they appear to me? They were like alternating currents in search of a magnetic field. She was entranced by her past; he abhorred his. She was dreamy and vague, he excitable and furious. When he came striding across Flint's lawn that first Saturday night he radiated so much energy she felt he might go up in smoke. And she recoiled. It was his vulnerability, not his force, that she was drawn to, and yet when his uncertainty manifested itself as rage—when he hurled his anger at the blocks of marble in the clearing on the top of the hill—she made light of it, put her hand on his and said, "There, there," as though he were a child awakening from a bad dream.

11

HERE IS MY Aunt Agatha describing their courtship:

"Your mother was the loveliest creature any of us had ever seen. Her eyes were deep-set, walnut-brown; you thought at first they were still, but when you came up close you saw they were always moving about, shimmying. Was it merriness or desperation? Everything else about her was so demure and calm, the way she held herself—your grandmother said, 'Sarah, stand up *straight*,' and so she had that frightful Starcliffe dignity. Even Arthur, who is really quite a tiny little thing, *seems* tall because of the way he stands and that habit you all have—you have it too, Peter—of tilting your chins. Are you really looking down your noses at us? I don't think your mother was. She was like a creature trying to break out of captivity, all covered up in long skirts and high-necked blouses. I would bring her some playsuits and dresses from the store and she would try them on and say, 'Goodness, Aggie, what am I going to wear *under* this?' And when I said, 'Not much, sweetie,' she turned bright red.

"Henry was bowled over. He'd call me up and start reading some awful poem he'd written, and I'd say, 'If you don't mind, dear, I think I can be spared your love letters.' 'Is it too corny, Aggie?' 'Well, if you want my advice, I would send her a Shakespeare sonnet.' 'I think she's probably already read those, don't you?' 'That's the point, Henry dear.' Poor eager old thing. You see, neither of them knew how to behave. They knew how to hold hands; that was about it. Your mother had hardly set foot out of that house. I don't think she'd gone out with a young man before. Ned Willoughby was a little in love with her. He was just taking over his father's medical practice. But she snubbed him. I suppose she wanted to get the hell out of there. So he upped and married another girl, a pretty young thing, except she drank too much. My God, the amount we drank! I gave your mother her first sip of gin. She seemed to like it, after a bit. I taught her how to hold a cigarette and at least *pretend* to smoke it—I wanted to loosen her up, and those parties at Flint's were made to order. We were starting our lives. We loved coming up from the city. The only person missing was Arthur. All that summer he stayed in New York. Henry was dying to meet him, and Sarah wanted Arthur to meet *him*. It created a kind of tension, his never being there, as though Sarah couldn't go beyond a certain point without his first knowing all about it.

"And then one weekend in early November he came up and all hell broke loose."

Arthur arrived late. His crisply pressed Dunhill suit, his subdued tie, his polished black shoes had a sureness that my father's and Flint's dress lacked. He had only been in the city for two years; but he was nearly forty years old, and he felt apprehensive whenever he returned to the valley. This was for him a place of disappointments. Memories came rushing back, but even worse was the realization that he had changed and it would show and somehow be held against him.

Flint's house was ablaze with lights. Arthur had expected

only a quiet evening with his brother and sister and perhaps a few old friends. The sight of the place all lit up this way, the sounds of music and laughter wafting out over the lawn, made him hold back, feeling very much a stranger.

"Ah, there you are!" shouted Flint as Arthur came in through the kitchen door. "My brother Arthur graces us with his presence this evening."

Flint rose from the card table, the sleeves of his shirt rolled up snugly against his upper arms and a green eyeshade pulled low over his forehead. Arthur, taking in the poker chips and cards and piles of change on the kitchen table, wondered if for his brother the whole world had not become a casino. That, from all accounts, was the way Flint conducted himself at work. He loved the hot tip, the quick gain, the bluff and the dare. Arthur wondered if his brother had the nerve that kind of life required; he knew *he* didn't; he preferred a safer course.

My mother took Arthur's arm and began introducing him around. The kitchen and the front parlor were crowded with young men and women standing close, smoking cigarettes and drinking country liquor. In the far corner of the parlor a small group had gathered at the piano. The mob parted a little as Arthur came through. As he shook hands he looked each person in the eye, trying to be open and friendly but feeling only stiff and contrived. He knew many of them from his childhood, but already their names had begun to slip away. He supposed there was some event—perhaps a day fishing along the river with one or two of them—that might help recapture some vestige of boyhood intimacy. But it seemed doubtful. He had run the Starcliffe Works, after all. That was what had first set him apart—more than going off to college, more than going off, afterward, to Wall Street, although he supposed they were all steps along the same path. Yes, he said when Flint approached with a glass, he would like a drink; yes, a whisky would be fine.

They approached the piano, where my father sang easily, flushed and boyish and obviously pleased with the sound of his voice. There was no reason to believe that Arthur had ever heard of Henry Kempton before; he was no more likely to have been told of my mother's beau than of Flint's parties. But my father knew about Arthur Starcliffe; he had heard the stories of his legendary work habits, his shrewdness, his rapid rise at the Grenfell firm. He was eager to talk to him, eager to make an impression. The singing stopped, and the two men shook hands, my father returning Arthur's stare with a wide-eyed look that had about it an element of defiance.

"Henry went to Yale," my mother said softly, trying to quiet an awful palpitation of her heart.

"Oh?" said Arthur. "What society were you in?"

My father let loose a burst of nervous laughter. My mother had not realized it was so loud. "Society? Why I suppose you could say I was in the laundry society."

Arthur smiled pleasantly and moved away.

My father, who thought he'd been quite witty, watched the older man, so cool and sure, slipping away, shaking other hands. Was this all the conversation there was to be? Crestfallen, he turned to the piano and reached for his drink. The singing started up again, but he did not join in.

Perhaps for my mother it was the moment when she looked over her shoulder and saw my father's disconsolate expression that the mood of the evening began to change. Or perhaps there was no particular moment—only a slow welling up of a feeling she had not been conscious of at these parties before. There were the usual number of people milling about, nearly fifty of them, the great majority of whom would spend the rest of their lives farming their families' land or working as clerks and merchants in the small towns along the Belledame. They came here each week to blow off steam, to talk of the experiences many of them had shared in the army. They were greatly drawn to Flint's affability; here they could get pleasantly plastered and sing songs and overlook the fact that among them some were moving away—indeed, a few, like Arthur and Flint and my father and Agatha, had already done so.

On this particular evening the liquor flowed as usual; food was served; after dinner some of them danced to the Gramophone. Arthur always seemed to be standing off to the side, looking on. The others glanced at him and then away. If he felt his isolation, they felt it too. Some of the men grew quiet and withdrawn; others became more boisterous, telling off-color stories and showing off like small boys trying to catch the attention of an indifferent father. Self-consciousness spread through the room like a stain.

My father's behavior was like that of the local boys, only more extreme. Arthur always seemed to touch a raw spot—first there was the question about the Yale societies; then he brought up the subject of the Kempton Marble Company, not exactly one of my father's favorites, and described how one day he had come here to Mercersville to see if the marble would be suitable for Clarence Starcliffe's gravestone. Lila Starcliffe had wanted something out of the Belledame Valley earth. "But of course it wasn't appropriate."

After supper my father dogged Arthur's heels. All he wanted was to establish contact. Why was Arthur making it so hard? He didn't seem to know much about the Stimson firm. My mother had the feeling he might not even have heard of it before; she could see this astonished my father, and there he was again, persistent as a terrier, planting himself beside the older man, asking him about the stock market the way he sometimes interrogated Flint, who loved playing the expert and quickly converted a prediction into a wager. But Arthur wasn't like that—didn't Henry see? Arthur was close-mouthed, and he wore his dignity the way a priest wears his robes, flowing out on all sides and creating a little necessary distance.

My father needed fortification and found it in gin. He was

like a hunter stalking a small but dangerous animal in a room thick with shouting and smoke and the foggy sounds of the phonograph's songs.

Over by the piano, Ned Willoughby's pretty raven-haired bride was sobbing. Ned leaned over to comfort her. "Don't touch me," she cried, "don't, Ned!" He threw an anguished look my mother's way; she stared at the girl, wondering how anyone could be as unhappy as *that*.

It was after midnight when Agatha came up to her, hiccuping and agreeably disheveled. "There's trouble brewing, sweetie. Our dear brothers do not exactly seem to be hitting it off."

From the porch came the sound of angry voices.

My mother and Agatha stood in the doorway. The two men were jaw-to-jaw, and my mother's first thought was, Oh, Arthur, be gentle. The Gramophone stopped; the voices in the parlor suddenly quieted down; people were pressing in from behind, trying to get a look. My mother wanted to block their view; she didn't want them to see; she could hardly bear it herself, the two men she cared for more than any in the world having an awful quarrel. Arthur saying now, in his most pedantic tone, "I will not have you pumping me. I don't know who you are, but I will not—"

"Pumping?" My father's eyes were like pale saucers. There were flaming spots in the middle of his cheeks. "Why, there isn't anything to pump."

"Get Flint," said my mother. She felt faint; she put out a hand to steady herself against the doorframe. "Oh, quick, Aggie, get him."

"It's all hot air. It's been pumped up as high as it will go, you little snot."

There was a roar of laughter from the parlor. Arthur was rigid as a post. My father began to weave—was he drunk, or did he expect to be struck? Arthur took a step forward, and my father brought his arm back and launched a tremendous swing. Flint came charging through the doorway and placed his tall frame between the two of them and took my father's blow on the shoulder. He gave him a little shove, then held him back against the railing of the porch, saying in a low voice, "Easy, tiger. Easy."

There was bedlam. The crowd came bursting out onto the porch. In a moment there were mock fistfights taking place out on the lawn. One man tackled another and down they went over the porch steps. A small group clustered around my father and began to strike him affectionate blows on the arms, but he twisted away and leaped the railing and was moving across the lawn. "Henry!" my mother cried, and she began to run after him. Arthur shouted, "Sarah, it's time we went home," and she called back, "No, Arthur, no!" and kept on going.

She caught up with my father and took his arm, and they walked along the empty dirt road, his silence testimony to his anger and self-reproach. He had spent the entire evening offering up his various tendernesses and gotten nothing in return. He was glad he had called Arthur Starcliffe a snot—glad and appalled too.

"Are you all right, darling?"

She had never called him that before. The word seemed to fling itself out into the brisk night air like a clarion call.

"That bastard."

"Oh, please don't. Please forgive him. For me."

But he did not reply. Instead he took her hand and held it, swinging their arms in short, stiff arcs.

She looked up at the panoply of stars; she breathed in the sharp November air—these were the things she wanted to remember. Soon the quarrel would be forgotten; it was one of those things that happen at a party, one of Flint's wild parties. But in her heart she knew she was fooling herself: Arthur and Henry were like frayed wires that had come into contact and started throwing off sparks. Her breath steamed in little clouds before her, and she kept thinking, Oh, please, forgive him. You don't understand what Arthur's been through.

She had been injured too; all her feelings were flowing out of her like tears, and she needed him to stopper them up. She had called him darling. Oh, why didn't he take her in his arms and kiss her?

And when they came in view of his family's house, when they came up on the front lawn and the noise of their walking stopped and the world was absolutely still, at that moment when she had almost given up, he turned to her and did.

12

A WEEK LATER he asked her to marry him. She felt a wild blossoming of pride and told him she would.

She rushed to tell her mother, who sat solemnly in her chair and said only that she must have Arthur's permission. Arthur was head of the family and would know what was best. My mother was mortified. She longed for her father; he would have embraced her and made the moment a celebration.

She wrote Arthur at once, telling him that she was "a grown woman with a heart and mind of my own. I am writing because Mother says I must. I trust you will do your sister the honor of giving her away."

He came up to Ellsworth Falls that weekend. She dreaded his arrival, and all her fears were confirmed when he told her, wearing his most determined expression, that he did not approve.

"What in the world can you mean, Arthur? You don't even know him."

Her cheeks blazed. She wished it were true—wished that Arthur didn't know him, wished that the dreadful episode on Flint's porch had never taken place.

"It's not what you are thinking, Sarah."

He had nothing against Henry Kempton personally—surely she must understand that. She was quite right—he still knew very little about him. But he had been investigating the firm he worked for and did not like what he had found. Peter Stimson was a clever man, some people thought too clever by far.

"I love *him*, Arthur, not his firm."

"These things are important, Sarah. I want you to marry someone we can trust."

It was a shocking thing to say. It made her wish that the whole thing were only a matter of Arthur's pride, as she had thought but a moment before. She could rebel against that; she could hurl his aggrieved pride back at him. But the Arthur sitting across from her now was steady and sure. He spoke calmly; she could hear the care in his voice. And these matters of business—what did she know of the way men behaved toward each other there? Was it really trustworthiness he was worried about? Or some delicate question of prestige? Her thoughts twisted back on themselves. Couldn't he see that her life was at stake?

He put his hand on her arm and said softly, "I'll talk to the boy."

Oh, why did he call him that—didn't he know that that was what they once called *him*?

"Talk, talk, talk all you want to. You won't talk him out of it—nor me." And she ran from the room.

When my father came uncertainly into the house, my mother went over and put her arms around him and kissed him on the mouth as though to bestow, in Arthur's presence, the gift of her affection and defiance. The two men went into a small back room. She stood leaning with her head against the door, feeling limp, half wishing to hear what they were saying, half wishing she could live in a silence as encompassing as her mother's. She stood there for a long time. Once she heard shouting—then, later, an odd burst of laughter. Good God, were they telling jokes?

The door opened. My father came out, saw her, smiled. He was very pale. Arthur put his arm around her shoulder.

"Sarah, I am very pleased. I believe we have come to an understanding."

"Oh, Arthur, thank you!" She had never thought there could really be any significant difference between them. She was immensely relieved; and grateful to Arthur for resolving the matter; and she vowed to put the whole thing out of her mind as quickly as she could.

Did she ever find out the nature of the bargain the two men had struck? Years later, under circumstances greatly changed, she asked Arthur what had taken place. But there was no urgency in her voice, no real curiosity about the matter. For while there were parts of the past that still held her in its grip, there were others she wished only to evade.

"I made Henry promise to leave the Stimson firm," said Arthur. "I made it clear that if he could not find a job elsewhere, he could come to work for us; that is, for me."

"That was all?" It was what she had thought at the time; the confirmation came as a relief.

"That was all. But Henry did not keep his promise." And there was in Arthur's voice such sadness and fatigue that she knew the promise and the breaking of it had been far more than her "all." It had somehow been at the heart of things—at the heart of what had begun in their lives and what was yet to come. And still she did not see it; once more she averted her gaze. She did not wish to see, and as it turned out, she never would.

13

IT WAS A small family wedding, a simple ceremony in the Episcopal church on the Main Street of Ellsworth Falls. Peter Stimson had given his protégé a smart Ford touring car as a wedding gift and had offered them his house on Long Island for their honeymoon. These things my father—wild with gratitude and excitement—accepted. Had he already forgotten his promise to Arthur? Or was he simply delaying the day of reckoning? If so, the reckoning would almost certainly be more severe.

After the flat sprawl of the city they found themselves roaring along the North Shore roads, passing through small villages and over bridges that spanned the sparkling inlets of the Sound. It was early May. They were dressed for spring, my mother in flowered silk and a broad-brimmed hat with a pink rose pinned to its crown. My father wore a linen suit, a Sulka kerchief in his breast pocket. Spring was laid out before them —forsythia, magnolia, cherry and apple had come bursting into bloom at once. They were delighted by the luscious unfolding countryside and the splendid estates etched sharply across the flat fields. And they were amazed at themselves. They kept looking at each other, exchanging loving glances, their innocence only enlarged by their first timid glimpses, the night before at the Plaza, of each other's naked limbs and flesh.

They came to Lamb Lane in Old Clarkstown. A black sign with gold lettering proclaimed *Excelsior*; below that, in smaller letters, *P. B. Stimson.* Dark hemlocks made a corridor; light came down through dappled sycamores. They rolled along cobblestones and turned after half a mile or so into a courtyard with high stone walls on three sides and the imposing facade of Peter Stimson's house on the fourth.

A cheerful pink-faced man with a thatch of white hair stood by the front door with a young boy. Had they been there all morning? Or had someone seen them coming and given a signal, like a sentry on a rampart in olden days?

"Good morning, madam. Morning, sir. My name is Joseph. This lad is Timothy."

They were led through a high-ceilinged hallway banked with massive settees and armoires. At the end of the room there climbed a crabbed staircase with a wrought-iron balustrade.

Maroon velvet fell like jowls from the canopy of the high oak double bed. Joseph went over to the windows and swung them open. My mother looked out over a glorious landscape, a lawn that sloped down to a pasture filled with sheep. The smell of blossoms and freshly mown grass filled the air.

Downstairs they wandered hand in hand through dark-paneled rooms. Glassy-eyed beasts stared at them from on high. In the library, over the cavernous stone fireplace, hung a portrait of their host astride a fine sorrel mare. There were a pair of Irish setters at the feet of the horse, and behind the equestrian figure a house could be seen, this house, a squarish, crenelated mass, but in the artist's foreshortening horse and rider dominated the scene, larger than the house, larger than the landscape itself.

My mother studied Peter Stimson's face. She knew almost nothing about him, except that he had come here from England and opened his firm; and when the war had ended and Henry had finished Yale, he had gone to work for him. Arthur had said that he was "too clever by far," but cleverness was not the quality conveyed by the rider in the portrait. There was sureness in the way he sat in the saddle; there was vigor. In another man the heavy body and the fleshy face might have suggested softness, but the bulk of this one made him only more forceful, almost imperious. He was lord of the manor, you could see that. My mother was a little frightened of him, and frightened too when they sat eating lunch in the formidable dining hall, samovars on the high sideboards and more animals staring from the walls. She was stunned by the blunt masculinity of the place.

After lunch they fell asleep side by side on the lawn. When they awoke they found that Joseph had covered them with blankets.

In the courtyard of the stable, broad doors swung open to reveal the silver grillwork of a mighty automobile. A darkly freckled man came toward them, wiping powerful hands on a cloth. "I'm Slater," he said pleasantly. "I groom the horses and the automobiles. Mr. Stimson said you and the missus—how do you do, ma'am?—might wish to go for a ride." He led them through another door; they went along a row of stalls, the horses dozing, tails swishing, the place smelling of manure and damp blankets and clovery meadows. "Darling," said my mother, "let's ride tomorrow before breakfast."

Joseph found him a pair of jodhpurs and boots.

"You look so dashing," she said as they walked along through the early morning dew.

A few minutes later he sat, white-knuckled, staring in astonishment at the strange creature moving about beneath him. My mother and Slater exchanged looks.

"Like me to go along, sir? I could show you the trails."

"That won't be necessary," said my father, trying to locate one of the stirrups.

"Are you sure, sweetheart?"

He shook his head; he was trying to position himself in the saddle, trying to steer the thing with his reins.

"Well, she's a gentle dear," said Slater. "Now look 'ere—"

he pointed—"you go down that woodland path a quarter of a mile or so and then you come out into the open. Let 'em canter a bit there." And he explained how they could make a circle, arriving back at "the big house" in about an hour, if that was enough for them on the first day.

They started off quickly through a grove of birch and maple. The horses were eager in the cool spring air, their hoofs striking small rocks one moment, sucking noisily into little pockets of mud the next. Their saddles made a lovely creaking sound.

"Take it a little more in the knees, Henry."

"I'm all right!"

They came out into an open space, and the horses took off in a brisk canter. A morning freshness lay on the land; a cloud of red-winged blackbirds fluttered up from the side of a marsh; the new leaves of the birch trees were bright green, the bark almost silver. My mother was enchanted; the uneasiness she had felt in Peter Stimson's house fell away. Looking back over her shoulder, eager to show and share her pleasure, she saw my father with his chin burrowed in his horse's mane. He was pulling himself up, making a great glowering effort, gathering the flopping reins in his fists and jerking on them. The horse bared its teeth; its ears went back and its front legs locked into place.

My father went flying.

Joseph knocked on their bedroom door. She was wanted on the telephone. It was their host.

"What's this I hear about our young man almost breaking his neck?" His voice was like a horn filled with saliva. It made her grip the phone harder, as though it were alive and might bite. "Is he all right, my dear?"

"He has a nasty cut. And Slater says a bit of a concussion. He's resting now."

It was like that moment when she had leaned over the unconscious body, the whole field suddenly immense and the light flat and pale. Who was this strange young man stretched out before her? What was she doing in this place? Who was that coming across the field toward them as fast as he could ride? The world seemed unreal. And now she felt it again in the library of this forbidding house, this rough voice assaulting her on the phone.

"Doctor Steiglitz is my personal physician. An excellent man. He's on his way out from the city to take a look. If he says I may, I should so like to visit our dear patient tomorrow."

But this was their honeymoon. She began to protest, but he went right on.

"I will ring off now, my dear. I hope I will have the pleasure of seeing you. My affectionate greetings to the dear, dear boy."

There was a roar of laughter and then: *click.*

The doctor sewed my father's scalp and gave him a sedative and suggested my mother sleep in the adjoining room. When she awoke the next morning she hurried to him, bursting in and exclaiming as she saw him sitting up and smiling, a breakfast tray in his lap, "Why, darling, you're better!" Then she saw the figure in the chair by the bed.

"The bride!" the voice roared. "You didn't tell me she was so lovely, Henry."

He was getting up from the chair—it was hard raising that formidable bulk—and came limping toward her. It was then she saw that he had a wooden leg. She hadn't known—why in the world hadn't Henry told her?

They stood and appraised each other—my mother, twenty-three years old, in a girlish nightdress and a piqué robe given to her by Agatha. Her long brown hair tumbled over her shoulders. Later my father said she looked gallant. It did not seem to her that gallantry should be called for. She saw before her a man of about forty—perhaps a bit older—who had grown quite stout. He was dressed in a tweed jacket and twill knickers, the artificial leg extending from the bunched cloth around the knee. He had a massive head, a bushy mustache, the same sharp eyes she had seen in the portrait, a little dab of red in the corner of one adding to the intensity of his gaze. He seemed to be daring her to size him up: Well, now, what do you make of me? She returned his stare. He was not the English country gentleman she had expected. English, yes, and country, maybe; but gentleman? No, he was more a peg-leg buccaneer on the deck of his ship, ready to run off with any cargo he could find. And Henry had been taken on as crew.

They sat facing each other across the bed, my father propped between them, a prince with a crown of bandages. Sunlight poured in. On a small table next to Stim stood a silver coffeepot with a glossy rattan handle, an upright rack of crustless toast, a jar of English marmalade. Joseph came in and placed a similar table next to her. The fresh coffee smelled delicious. She sipped from a dimpled white cup, quietly observing her new husband and the pride Stim took in him, and feeling her hostility soften. If this powerful brute cared for the man she loved, then there was already a bond between them. But still, she had not exactly expected to find Henry's employer and his butler in their bedroom on the third morning of their honeymoon. And though she wanted to laugh at it—perhaps in years to come she would—she could not quiet the tug of resentment.

"Did it run smoothly?" she heard Stim ask. "Oh, it was grand," said my father, "wasn't it, Sarah?" They were talking about the new car—a child's toy, she realized, next to the elegant beauty in the garage.

"And how is that clever brother of yours?" Stimson burst

into laughter; his grumbles and guffaws made her feel he was expiring from an unexplained attack of mirth. "Oh, Arthur Starcliffe's made a name for himself! Quite remarkable, considering that Percy Grenfell likes a bit of the limelight too. I have been longing to meet him." He fixed her with his penetrating gaze. "Perhaps I shall soon have that pleasure."

My father cast an anxious look in my mother's direction. She could not understand why suddenly the color had drained from his face.

She thought really it was time for their host to go. But he sat like a leviathan; and little by little the conversation moved away from her. It was no longer a conversation, but a kind of chant; they were like members of a tribe exchanging messages she didn't understand. Stimson pulled a sheaf of papers from his breast pocket and put them on the bed. "Take a look at these, Henry, will you?" saying it agreeably, with only a hint of command, and she knew that for them she was no longer in the room, she was like Joseph, a phantom who kept slipping in and out. She realized then that Henry's accident had provided a pretext for Stimson's arrival. He would have come anyway—perhaps not into their bedroom, perhaps not quite this soon, but surely within a day or two. The only question was, how long would he stay? She looked at the window with an immense sense of longing, and a few seconds later she slipped away. When she stood in the hallway and heard their voices going on, she knew they had not noticed; she had simply disappeared.

Slater saddled one of the mares, and she went off across the flat countryside, taking the fences. It was glorious—she wanted to ride and ride, all the way back to Ellsworth Falls. But when she and her horse came walking slowly back through the woods, her exhilaration was gone. Only her longing to escape remained, and it filled her with shame. Perhaps she was a spinster at heart. She wondered if she should have stayed at her mother's side, mending and sewing and playing cards and keeping the old woman company for the rest of her days. Her cowardice appalled her. How could she be so timid, so unsure, when such a short while ago she had longed only to leave home?

"Henry, what is he *doing* here? Doesn't he know it's our honeymoon? Of course he knows. Damn him, damn, damn, damn!"

"Sarah, he likes us."

"*Likes* us? What an odd way to show it! And why didn't you tell me about his leg?"

"I'd forgotten. One gets used to it, you'll see. He'll tell you the story—he loves to tell it, about how he lost it in China."

"China? God, what a preposterous man!"

On their last day Stimson gave a farewell party. Just before joining the other guests for lunch, my father went over to my mother and put his arms around her. She was standing before a full-length mirror adjusting the sash on her dress.

"We'll be alone soon, Sarah."

"Are you sure, darling?"

"We'll have the apartment to ourselves."

"We won't have to come back, will we, Henry?"

He turned away in distress and stood with his hands on the sill of the window looking out over the lovely countryside. "Does this really make you so unhappy?"

The two of them stood together. Now it was she who had her arm on his shoulder.

"He *scares* me."

"Stim?" He burst out laughing. "Why, he's the kindest man in the world. Look what he's done for us."

Feeling his enthusiasm, she held her ingratitude in close; she must never let it show. "I'm such a ninny," she said. "I've never been anywhere. I don't understand these things."

"But I don't either." He beamed at her, as bright and eager as the first time she had seen him coming across Flint's lawn. "But I want to find out. We'll find out together."

They turned toward each other. She kissed him, a slow, lingering kiss the ardor of which took her by surprise. She had done it, really, to calm herself, but she saw now that he took it for complicity.

When, rosy-cheeked and happy, Stim raised his champagne glass, she smiled at him and then at my father, and there could be no question of how surely the three of them were bonded. "Our beautiful bride!" Stim roared. "To our Sarah!" And after lunch when they took their glasses out on the lawn, she marveled at how kind they were, the men in their Harris tweeds and splendid waistcoats, the women in their demure dresses—they were all so jovial and sweet. Shortly, Joseph announced that the car was ready. The guests followed them round the corner of the house to the front courtyard. Glasses were lifted again—Godspeed! Happy journey! Long life! Come back soon! And then the car was rattling over the cobblestoned driveway, the sun shining down through the dappled sycamores; it was as lovely as when they had first come to this place a few days before. If there were more shadows in my mother's heart, she kept them hidden, and when they went through the gate, passing Stim's sign, she thought Henry would burst with pride. "Excelsior!" he shouted giddily. She smiled at him, touched his arm, leaned her head against him. She wanted him to know that they had drunk of the cup together and that she shared his joy.

14

"FLINT HAD ALL his customers on margin. Do you know what margin is, sweetpea? Do they teach you that at Harvard?"

I was lying on the living-room floor of my Aunt Agatha's Gramercy Park apartment, visiting New York on a spring weekend during my junior year. Life was beginning to stare me in the face that May. Wrestling with the mystery of what had gone wrong between my parents, I found I could not always stare back. And so I had come to my aunt for help.

She sits on her brown velvet sofa in a loose-fitting robe, peonies on a black silk background, the kind of flamboyant costume I found hideous in my childhood but which I have recently come to see has—like Aggie's painted Chippendale highboys and Moroccan throw rugs and Kandinsky lithographs—a devil-may-care style. She has spent her life working for Birnbaum's department store and as a head buyer knows how to shop. She knows where to purchase Chinese lacquer and Italian leather; she knows when there will be an auction of Expressionist drawings or a sale of Dutch bulbs. She pores through newspapers for announcements of bargains or forthcoming musical events, smoking one cigarette after another, crushing the butts in glazed black dishes from Oaxaca. She strokes her cat; applies rouge; answers the phone; proffers advice on the theater, on corsets, on tenors, on automobiles, on love affairs.

"Of course your Uncle Arthur saw 1929 coming, and made a killing. But Flint was out on a limb. So Arthur *banished* him. He sent him up to Mercersville and he's supported him ever since. Better *that* than the possibility of disgrace. Flint's an old country boy anyway; he hasn't been so miserable up there, has he now?"

She shoos her cat away and gets up and rummages in a drawer. At the other end of the living room, lime-green lovebirds chatter in a standing gilt cage. Aggie comes back to the sofa with a folder. "Here, what do you think of these?" And she hands me a photograph of my mother, staggeringly young, dressed in a knit suit with full sleeves, very French. Her hair clings to her head like a ruffled cap, revealing one small ear, the lobe blazingly white. Her eyebrows make marvelous dark lines across her pale skin; she is looking down almost seductively at a cigarette held in slender fingers. Then Aggie shows me my father and Stim standing before a tennis net. Stim has a kerchief knotted across the top of his forehead. The two of them have won a match—you can see victory in my father's eyes and in the way he holds his racket high. Stim has his arm around him.

"Well?" says Aggie.

Whether we have just come from Carnegie Hall or the Trans-Lux, this is what she says: *Well?* And then she is off on a discourse of her own, full of enthusiasm or invective, and we dash along, her hand on my arm, steering me toward the nearest Longchamps. But now she waits and watches. I am moved by these photographs, my mother and father young and handsome and somehow still *clear*. They make me want to weep; but I do not display my emotion, I say only that they were both "beautiful."

"Were? They still are. Just because you are almost grown up, do not think that your parents cease to have looks or charm."

"I didn't know my mother was so soignée."

"Oh, she wasn't, sweetpea. I never saw her hold a cigarette like that in my life. She was playacting, poor dear."

In those early days, she tells me, my father was always drunk. "Oh, not on whisky or gin. He was drunk on convertible debentures and underwriting syndicates. He was drunk on work; he was sodden, tipsy—he couldn't talk or think of anything else. Like all the young men, he went to the office six days a week; and on Sunday he and your mother drove to Excelsior to go horseback riding and have lunch. 'Oh, Aggie,' she used to complain, 'Stim's got him all week—and then on Sundays too.' "

They lived in an apartment on the top floor of a house in Brooklyn Heights. When my sister, Susan, and my brother, Randolph, were born, Fräulein Merz came to stay. She organized the household and marched the two children up and down the Esplanade in all kinds of weather. Suddenly my mother felt idle—Aggie could see it. Aggie lived around the corner in those days and would pop in for a drink several times a week; on Saturdays she took my mother to museums and concerts.

"I was the only friend she had, ducky. She didn't seem to *want* friends. Up until then her brothers had been her friends, but now Flint was playing in bridge tournaments and Arthur—why, Arthur always made her feel that he was watching her, watching her marriage, waiting for it to come apart. She was already lonely. There are many women like her; they come to the city with their ambitious husbands and there isn't anything for them to do; or they don't know how to find it; or for some reason they don't want to. I was lucky, you know. I came on my own."

"But Aggie, what about my father and Arthur? Why did they hate each other so?"

She brushes cigarette ash from her robe and holds up her sherry glass for me to fill. The lovebirds chatter away, and through the open windows comes the pleasant sound of Sunday morning traffic. When my aunt resumes, her voice has lost a little of its bounce; she is more unsure and says, "I only wish I knew, sweetie," but after she has lit another cigarette and is settling down to her sherry she tries to explain about Arthur, about how he liked to tie life up in neat little packages labeled "Arthur Starcliffe. Mine." Only my father wouldn't be tied.

"They're alike in some ways, even though they can't bear to be in the same room. And then Arthur couldn't abide Stim. Arthur's a man of will; he's gotten ahead in life because of stamina, not imagination. Stim had *flair*. Stim had *feelings*. You could always talk to Stim about a painting or a garden or a book."

When I point out that my mother never thought so, Aggie gives a whoop of laughter. "Your mother was ornery! She'd come home from Stim's in a tizzy and say, 'Aggie, I don't know for the life of me whether that man has taste or just a big pocketbook.' And I'd jump on her. What difference does it make? I ask you. We all buy our taste sooner or later. Some of us buy it with time, some with money. At least in my humble world no one confuses reality with aesthetic pretension. We know we are dealing with chattels."

At Lüchow's my aunt wears a toque with a lavender feather; there are more feathers—a silver boa—around her neck. Lumpy turquoise stones hang down over her olive sweater, which is tight across her ample bosom. She is having a Manhattan, and we are eating gravlax with dill sauce. She is downing food and drink with great enthusiasm, and I am struck by her bountiful enjoyment of life. Impulsively I ask her why she has never married. Surely she was more genuinely "marriageable" than my elusive and puzzling mother.

My aunt blushes. "What a question, ducky."

She is so strong and direct that I feel she must be invulnerable. But I am wrong. She is hurt, and I am surprised.

"There have been a number of . . . possibilities. I have been in love in my time, if you can believe it."

"Oh, Aggie, of course I believe it."

An orchestra starts tuning up in one of the other rooms. A louvered door swings to and fro as the waiters come from the adjoining bar with mugs of beer. The place smells of malt and of mushrooms and of Agatha's rather heavy perfume.

"The damned trouble was—the trouble *is*," she says, "the men I am truly interested in, the ones who can think and who can talk, I can't for the life of me fall in love with. And the ones I fall in love with, the ones who *move* me, the ones I want to *hold*"—I am amazed; her old, powdered face is blushing—"they *stupefy* me. You wake up in the morning and there they are and what in the world does one do with them? I feel I have to see them in shifts. It has to do with the specialization of labor, I suppose. You see, the only person I really care for and am interested in too—is *me*!"

"That's the way I feel about you too, Aggie."

"Then *you* marry me, sweetpea. I'll lay on a car and a driver and we'll go down to Maryland right after lunch for a quickie."

The waiters come and go, bringing Wiener schnitzel and red cabbage and German fried potatoes. "My, how glorious," says Agatha. "We must have a Piesporter to wash this down."

The orchestra begins to play a Viennese waltz.

"What I don't understand," my aunt says with sudden and unexpected vehemence, "is why your mother didn't *fight* for your father. She just folded her tent. Took one look at that clever, beautiful woman and fled the field of battle. I don't know why. Your mother has courage. She has spirit."

"Perhaps she never really loved him."

"Loved him? She adored him!"

This does not fit my picture of things. I tell my aunt of the sound of their voices coming up to my bedroom through all the years of my childhood—voices so edgy and angry that I put my pillow over my head to block them out.

"Quarrels? They mean we're still alive, that we still care. Why, I remember a time—it was before you were born—

when your father was so furious with your mother that he struck her. That was years ago. And they went on together, didn't they? For a long, long time."

I have already heard my mother's version of this episode, but I do not let on. I want to hear my aunt tell it. And after taking a bite of cheesecake she begins to describe my father coming home to the Brooklyn Heights apartment in a state of great excitement.

" 'You here, Aggie? Good. I've got news. Let me fix a drink first.'

"I was sure he'd been promoted or fired. I see it all the time at the store. People go berserk. Either way, I knew it must be pretty important, for usually he blurted things straight out; it wasn't like him to go and mix a cocktail first. He wanted to keep your mother and me in suspense.

"And when he came back into the room he said, 'Stim has given us a wonderful piece of land. We rode over it last weekend. Remember, sweetheart? He didn't let on for a second, did he? Now he's given it to us.'

"Your mother was horror-struck. Your father said that Stim wanted them to start building immediately. They were to use George Devane as their architect. 'He's the best.' You know how your father is about the best. The best restaurant, the best resort, the best automobile—it intoxicates him. Your mother said it was absurd, how could they possibly afford a fancy house? But your father had the answers: Stim was going to advance him some funds against his share of the firm's profits. Your mother went over to the window—there was a splendid view of the harbor—and leaned her head against the cool pane, and I could tell she was looking down at the boats and wishing she could get aboard one of them and sail off to the ends of the earth. Your father was going on and on. It was to be a Georgian house. There was an old orchard they could cut down to make a fine lawn. It was clear he and Stim had given the whole thing a lot of thought. And your mother's back seemed to drive him wild. This was the most important moment in his life. And at last she turned slowly and looked at him and said, 'Oh, will you be quiet.' And then, with great firmness: 'I won't go. I won't live next door to that man.'

"She moved toward him as if to emphasize her determination. She looked astonishingly beautiful; her dark eyes glowed, she was absolutely serene. It was more than your father could bear. He stepped forward and hit her with the back of his hand—hit her across the mouth and drew a trickle of blood. She stood looking at him as though nothing had happened. You must never think, Peter, that they weren't a fine match.

" 'Of course you'll go,' said your father. 'You're my wife.' When she didn't reply, he said, 'All right. I'll go without you.'

"It was then I spoke up. 'I'm the one who's going. Right now. Sarah, take my handkerchief. You've got blood all over your chin. You're going to have a swollen lip. Henry, fetch some ice.'

" 'Like a drink for the road, Aggie?'

" 'What, a drink from a brute like you?'

" 'Come off it, Agatha.'

" 'Does he often treat you like this, Sarah? Does my brother *molest* you?'

"Then your mother said the most astounding thing, Peter. She said, 'Only when I've got it coming to me, Aggie,' and she rushed forward and fell into your father's arms, sobbing."

When we are out on the street again, I confess to my aunt that I have heard the story before, only in my mother's version the entire episode is a little absurd. I tell Agatha how my mother would burst out laughing; she would slap her thigh and exclaim, "Your father was perfectly ferocious, you know!" And then more softly, more gently, she would always add, "Of course we quickly made up. Why, that was the night you were conceived."

My aunt stops in her tracks and appears to be counting.

"Yes, it's altogether possible. And how old were you when she first told you this?"

"Nine or ten. Of course I didn't have the slightest idea what she meant."

"But how like her. What an extraordinary thing to tell a child." And she throws her hands up, almost in a gesture of supplication. "Oh, Peter, why has she gone so far away? Do you think she will ever come back to us again?"

PART
II

15

I AM BORN. Peter Stimson Kempton is my name. My godfather comes in his silver Bentley to the hospital in Brooklyn where my mother lies exhausted after the difficult birth. He presents my father with a gold-embossed savings passbook. An account has been established in my name in the amount of one thousand dollars. My father is exceedingly pleased. My mother's eyes are closed and she makes no response.

Our new house—the one my parents have fought over so ardently—is born when I am, and it is hard to say which birth is the more difficult. Susan and Randy and Fräulein greet us when we come up the driveway in my father's new Packard sedan. Susan cries out, "Oooh, look how small and ugly he is! Can I hold him? Please, Mama."

"Not now, dear. Here he is, Fräulein. At last." And she hands me to Fräulein, who clutches me to her puny bosom and coos.

The house soars overhead. It is a classic Devane house: Georgian, red-brick, with black shutters flanking the handsome six-paned windows that cross its facade. At the front entrance there is a circular portico with columns; a frieze of carved wooden rosettes frames the door. My mother's heart sinks as she stands by this doorway and surveys the scene. In their rush to finish, the workmen have left broken brick and lumber strewn across the grounds. The lower branches of the nearest trees are shattered. She has no sense of a new beginning or even of renewal, only of an army that has come through, wreaking havoc.

From the chaise longue in her bedroom she studies the

savaged landscape and notes with growing affection the dilapidated old apple trees out in back. It is then that she christens the place and commissions an elegant black-and-gold sign of the sort found all over the North Shore. Ours proclaims: *Apple Tree Farm. H. Kempton.* When my father hears her describe the place as "our apple farm," he grimaces. He wants something more elegant, like the names attached to the neighboring estates—Coe Manor or Arden Hills or Excelsior. He doesn't wish people to think he owns a simple farm—especially if it *isn't* one. It rankles him and amuses my mother, who plays it for all it's worth.

In the early spring she sets to work. The apple trees are pruned. Nurserymen bring truckloads of manure. Then come the bundled lilac, forsythia, quince, hemlock and yew. She plants wisteria against the house to "quiet" the brick. Two rows of copper beech line the driveway (someday, she says, it will be a grand "avenue"). Little by little this spring and the next and the one after that the grounds take on the shapes she has imagined in her head; it becomes a place of bright and dark paths, of rough and smooth surfaces, of dazzling and muted colors. She imagines gardens by Bonnard and Monet, glowing fields and startling pools of running purple light.

I am lying on a wool blanket. I can lift my head, rock on my elbows. The blanket scratches my chest and crotch. Rough hands spread oil on my shoulder and work their way down to my buttocks. There are two voices, the clumsy one, close, the person leaning over applying the oil; the other smoother, softer, farther away. Fräulein. Mama. They look down and laugh. I crane my head, but they are too high up to be caught in my line of vision. The voices, the laughter go away. I am alone on the rough blanket and want to get off it. I strain and push on my knees and then I am in motion—across the blanket and onto the grass, which is soft and a little wet. I come to the wall of the house. Cool earth. I sit up and scrabble at the earth and bring a handful to my mouth, smearing some of it across my face. Gray muck protrudes from a ridge of mortar. I reach for it. It crumbles and slender brown petals come flying out, darting and swirling. And they hurt my shoulders and neck and ears. I scream until my lungs break. Fräulein rushes to me. *"Mein Gott!"* she cries, folding me in her apron. The petals swarm around her too, stinging, stinging, stinging.

I take the two little kittens—no bigger than balls of yarn—and carry them, first one, then the other, to the edge of the wall and drop them over. They make no sound as they hit the low border of African violets. They lie still on the ground, just as still as in the basket. They lie curled up like snails. I walk down to fetch them, to drop them again.

"Here, here—what's going on here, *what are you doing*?"

It is my mother coming around the corner of the house. I see her and run into the pine trees.

"Come back here, young man. Come back this instant."

I cower and linger and hide. Why did I want to hurt the kittens? I don't know. I cannot imagine why.

Slowly the world changed. The wisteria climbed the red-brick walls of the house; the apple trees blossomed and bore fruit.

It changed; and it came into focus, as though someone had turned the ring of a telescope and the blurring, swimming universe emerged sharp, distinct, breathtaking. Sounds came wafting into my bedroom on summer days: the sprinkler hitting the side of the house like a ruffle of applause; Tony, our gardener and chauffeur, raking the driveway; the horses snorting and sneezing in the new stables. Blue, the setter, whined at the front door, wanting to get in; a little later he whined again, anxious to be outside.

As soon as I was old enough to swim, my father built a swimming pool. Tony was given the extra burden of keeping it clean. It made him more morose than before; he spent long hours at the edge of the woods, smoking and staring in the direction of the kitchen. From the apartment over the garage where he lived with his wife, Renata, came remarkably strong smells.

"Garlic," said my mother.

"Whisky," said my father. "Renata and Tony drink. It isn't a pleasant odor."

"Wop armpit," whispered my brother Randy, digging an elbow into my rib cage.

"I like Tony."

"We all like Tony," said my father, "and as long as he doesn't drink while he's driving the automobiles or tending the horses, I couldn't care less."

It was one of my father's clarifications.

It was a world of strict regimes. Fräulein knocked on our doors at precisely six-thirty each morning except Sunday, when another hour of sleep was allowed. Meals took place "on the dot." Each of us had a silver napkin ring and a jar of polish and a cloth with which to keep the ring shiny. There was, for every occasion, a mystifying and burdensome code known as "proper dress."

There were carefully specified chores—a correct way to do every little thing. We were commended for the task well done and on rare occasions our allowances—dispensed by my father at his dressing-room bureau on Sunday mornings—were supplemented by a small stipend, as though we were not really children at all but subcontractors who helped keep the household running in an orderly manner. The bowel movement was much worshiped and discussed. Periodically Fräulein inspected our stools, vouchsafing the consistency of these remarkable extrusions. If all else failed—inspections, exhortations, purges, enemas—we were delivered into the hands of Dr. Edgar Southworth on Park Avenue. In his quiet office he kneaded our bellies with gentle hands as though coaxing notes from the trembling strings of a lyre.

In this comfortable but regimented setting the hierarchy of my affections grew clear. An assortment of gerbils, hamsters, white rabbits and my English setter, Blue, ranked at the top. My pony, Stout, qualified when he was in his stall, cozying up to me with his rough nose. But when I climbed him and we headed out through the woods on our Sunday rides with my father and Stim, all thought of friendship was forgotten. Off the two men went at breakneck speed; I was never sure of staying on, never sure that Stout would not lock his heels and send me flying over his thick neck as my father had gone flying on his first ride years before.

Next in order of comradeship came Fräulein and Tony. For when Susan and Randolph—eight and six years older than I—went away to school, my father traveled more often, sometimes taking my mother along, and I was left with these two. I dogged their steps, indoors and out. Sometimes the three of us sat in the kitchen, Tony smoking and Fräulein bringing him cup after cup of coffee. On her days off Fräulein took me to the city, where we would have lunch in the glass-and-chrome interior of the Automat, and then high in the uppermost balcony of Radio City Music Hall thrill to the reverberations of the mighty organ. From these moments came an attachment that had to do with the accessibility of hands and arms and cheeks. Their accented voices, their clumsy bodies, their rough surfaces—all these strangenesses deepened my relief when I fled to them for comfort. They were substantial, and one could rub against their edges and be made to feel whole.

Stim and Randolph came next. They were confidants. I could tell them my secrets. If only I had had more. But as I grew older my awareness of their *force*—my brother's courage and my godfather's power—tinged my love with the tartness of respect.

My sister Susan? By the time I was ten years old, she was eighteen and away in college. Are there wider gulfs than that? When she came home I could not embrace her the way I embraced my brother; she had become not so much awesome as incomprehensible, not so much worldly (I see now) as female.

And then there were my mother and father.

If we come to see ourselves as small painted figures in a landscape, then my father was anxious that the landscape not be too vast and that his place in it be secure. There must be fixed and clearly marked boundaries—a solid frame for the painting of which he was part. Here was a man, after all, who loved timetables and stock market listings, who adored croquet and tennis, who dressed with a kind of snappy precision—there were stripes in his ties and gold buttons on his blazer, and a fine shine to his shoes. But if he was to be truly secure, he must know where the rest of us stood too. We must be fixed in place, just so. We must, above all, be measured for our achievements. We must catch the ball, ride the horse, earn the grade.

And my mother—how in the world place her? It would have been one thing if she had felt confined by the frame of the painting, if she had wished to smash that solid shining thing my father was trying to put up around us. But her discontent was not of that sort. She wished instead to break through the surface of the canvas itself, to go deeper into life, to a different kind of place.

My mother and father came last.

16

FOR HIS FIFTEENTH birthday my father gave my brother Randolph a watch. It was a splendid object with a buffered stainless-steel exterior and, best of all, a stopwatch hand that could be triggered by a small chrome plunger next to the winding mechanism.

Gathered at the dining-room table, we watched my brother open his presents. When he came to the slender box and pushed aside the tissue paper, he gave my father a dazzling smile. But the smile did not last. As he examined the watch more closely, disappointment spread across his face. My father saw it; his pleasure evaporated too. It did not return when Randy said grudgingly, "Thank you very much, Father. It's a lovely gift."

Exactly one hour after lunch the two of us stood by the side of the swimming pool. Randy took off the watch and laid it on the roped surface of the diving board. The sun caught its bright face and made it shine like a splendid gem. If for some reason my brother found it wanting, I did not. I longed to pick it up and feel the weight of it in my hand. I waited for him to tell me what was wrong, but he just looked down and hummed away in an enclosed and angry mood. Finally I asked him what the trouble was.

He and my father had paid a visit to Abercrombie & Fitch. They had looked at a number of watches, Randy making it clear that he needed a waterproof model to time his practice laps at the Grover pool.

"That was the whole point. *Comprenez?* But guess what? The waterproof models cost maybe fifteen bucks more. We looked at them anyway—a whole case full. And then he went back a couple of days later and bought this one. Can you believe it? He just couldn't go all the way—not even after getting my hopes up. Stingy bastard. I suppose he felt he couldn't afford it. After all, look at this dump." And together we looked at the pool and the fine soaring house. "Oh, hell, let's swim."

So we swam and ducked each other in the water and played tag, Blue dashing around the pool with us, round and round, the sun letting loose a flood of summery light from the deep sky. I kept glancing at the watch, hoping Randy would want to try it out. I offered to time him, if he wanted to swim some laps.

"Don't worry, squirt, you'll get your greasy paws on it soon enough." He dove back into the pool and began swimming underwater. I took hope from his words. If he could not use the watch at Grover, perhaps he would leave it with me.

I heard the screen door slam up at the house. It was like a revolver shot. My father came striding down the grassy embankment. I could tell from his walk and the set of his jaw that he was in one of his "serious" moods. He stopped by the side of the pool and, just as Randy's head broke the surface of the water, held up a piece of paper. "Randolph, what is the meaning of this?"

My brother hoisted himself out of the water and sat for a moment breathing heavily. Then he got up and studied the paper in my father's outstretched hand.

"It's a bill from the pro shop at the club." Still breathing heavily, he said in a slightly singsong way, "It shows a charge of twenty-five dollars for a racket, six dollars for a lesson, two dollars for two cans of balls."

"It's the racket that interests me."

My brother picked up a towel from the grass and began

drying himself, hopping on one foot to clear the water from his ears. He put the towel down and reached over to the diving board and picked up the watch, held it to his ear, and then kept it in his hand, his thumb rubbing its shining face. The sun beat down on the three of us, Father perspiring heavily in an open-necked shirt and long trousers. Blue lay panting at his feet.

"Did you purchase a new racket, Randolph? Without consulting me?"

"My old one broke."

"Did it, now?"

"Yes, sir. In the middle of my lesson."

"And so you bought a new one for twenty-five dollars?"

"Mr. Beazeley said it was the very best money could buy. It has Argentinian sheep gut and it's endorsed by Tilden."

I couldn't tell whether my father was angry because of the extravagance or the breach of financial etiquette. Or both. The bill from the club shook in his hand. Randy was trembling a little too, his lips purple and his teeth chattering, even though the sun was hot and there wasn't a touch of breeze. His thumb kept working the face of the watch.

"I thought you wanted me to play."

"That is not the point."

"Then what is the point?" He was making a tremendous effort to control himself. Blue, the dumb mutt, lay on the grass looking up adoringly at my father—the way he did when someone was about to throw a ball. "I was having a lesson, my racket broke, the pro sold me another one. The lesson was all right? You do want me to have lessons?"

I did not like the expression on my father's face. My legs felt weak, and my heart was beating so hard I could feel the vibrations in my neck. If there was anything worse than being extravagant, it was being *fresh*, and Randy, fighting for his life, was coming perilously close.

"If you do not understand the point, Randolph," my father said in his awful, slow way, "if you do not understand the meaning of money, and it seems to me this is not the first time today you have indicated to me that you do not, then I think you had better go to your room and stay there until you can tell me that you do."

"Go to my room?"

Now he was really shaking, and in his face I saw the first possibility of tears. I knew what I would have done—I would have burst out crying and run. I marveled at the way he stood his ground.

"You heard me."

"Now?"

It was his birthday. He looked up at the wonderful sky; he looked at me and the bright water of the pool. The thought of imprisonment on such an afternoon—for an incomprehensible crime such as this—seemed aberrant. And it was a punishment fit only for a child, the kind of thing they would do to *me*, not to Randy, who had been away at school for two years. He was mortified. It was what my father clearly intended, for you could see he felt better. His mouth had relaxed, his hand no longer shook. I did not understand what made grown-ups feel so pleased after they had inflicted pain. My father was really quite sure of himself now. He reached out and put his hand on Randy's shoulder and turned him, trying to propel him toward the house.

"March," he said, as Fräulein would have said to me.

Randy squirmed from under his grasp and stood on the marble apron of the pool. He did not march; he did not move at all. In that bright afternoon there was not a single sound, not the drone of an airplane or the whinnying of a horse or the familiar soughing of Tony's rake. Randy had a wild look, as though he were daring my father to come after him.

"All right, Father."

I was sure he meant, "All right, Father, you win," and I felt a welling up of relief and shame. It was over, this struggle, but it had ended in defeat. I was defeated too.

But still he did not move. He turned to me and gave me an odd smile, almost a smirk, and he looked at my father and for a moment I thought he was going to wink. And then he lifted his watch and held it high over the water, dangling it at the end of his outstretched arm.

"I called Mother from the pro shop," he said quietly. "I called about the racket and she said it was fine. She said to put it on our account and she would talk to you about it."

And then as my father and I, curiously and unexpectedly allied, looked on, he let the watch go. It hit the surface of the water, making the tiniest of splashes.

"Oh, Randy," I cried. It would never be mine now.

My father, stricken and pale, let the invoice from the club flutter to the grass. Smiling, Randolph brushed by him on his way to his room. Blue went after him.

17

UNLIKE MY BROTHER Randolph I made no effort to reach out to grasp the world, to challenge it, or in some infinitesimal way to shape it to my own ends. I went about my days dutifully, getting up quickly at Fräulein's knock, eating my abundant breakfast, waiting in one of a succession of gray Buicks until my father emerged from the house in a dark suit, a rust-colored briefcase under his arm. If he was on schedule, I would be dropped off at school on his way to the train. If he was late, I would be dropped off afterward, which meant I was late too, and had to walk down the long center aisle of the school's auditorium suffering my classmates' disdainful stares. In the late afternoon Tony fetched me, and after a brief interlude at home I went with him to greet my father at the train.

We sat together in the front seat. While we waited I read comic books and Tony thumbed his way through the sports and funny pages of the early edition of the *Journal-American*. Sometimes he got out of the car to smoke a small cigar, not wanting my father to find the interior reeking of its fumes. Sometimes I got out and ran my hand along the pleasing Simonized surface of the fenders and hood. There were a dozen or so other cars parked next to the station, most of them more elegant, their chauffeurs more nattily dressed than Tony, who wore work pants and a white shirt, with only his black visored cap to indicate that he had moved, officially, from the realm of the garden and stable to transportation. From time to time a train came in, a shuddering, hooting engine spouting cinders. After each train pulled out Tony reached into the glove compartment for a rag and briskly wiped cinders from the surface of the car. Other chauffeurs did the same. We usually had to wait for three or four trains until my father arrived, and during this wait I became aware of a growing anxiety.

What was I afraid of, waiting there? Was I afraid of him? Afraid that I had not been dutiful enough in the performance of my chores? Afraid because I knew my dutifulness was fraudulent—that I used it as a shield to hide my cowardice? Certainly I did not ask myself such questions then; I may not have even been aware of my anxiety as more than a fleeting thing—a concern, perhaps, that my father might be tired and in a bad mood at the end of his day. Why, then, does it come back to me now so vividly? Because I know the feeling still, sitting in my house by the river. I realize with a start that the connective tissue that links past with present is not the embroidered surface of memory and imagination, but this *feeling*. And while it comes back less frequently now, it is still what makes me turn to find solace in the roughness of bark and leaf and the feel of small precious objects, the soft rush of the river over smooth stones.

At last my father arrived, his step heavy and his face bleary with fatigue as he moved across the station platform.

I knew the place that he came from, for I had been taken on a visit to his office (his "orifice," my mother called it). Miss Boomer, his secretary, met me in the cavelike vestibule and took me up to the fifth floor in an old-fashioned lattice-work elevator. As we climbed I saw somber men sitting behind a wire-mesh screen; they wore green eyeshades, and the moving elevator threw bold stripes across their suits.

"That is the Cage," Miss Boomer said. "That is where we count the securities."

The walls of the partners' room were chocolate-brown. The partners sat in two rows of rolltop desks, their backs to us, their heads peering down at piles of documents. I saw thick, carefully brushed hair, bald spots, pink ears, gleaming collars. From a small fireplace came the tart smell of coal. It was like a schoolroom, only a dismal one, with no windows and no horseplay. Stim was shouting in an adjoining room.

"Your father is with Mr. Stimson," said Miss Boomer. "He'll be along in a minute. How do we look now?" She gave a tug at my tie, straightened it. "We look fine."

And then Stim was in a doorway, shouting, "Where is my godson? Stop moping there, Boomer, show him in. And bring us some tea. Peter and I will have a spot of tea, Henry, while you make those calls."

My father went by, hardly aware of me. Stim took me to his desk, let me spin in his chair and open the tiny drawers where he told me he kept his "secrets."

"Eesa here," Tony muttered, getting out the cloth for one last swipe at the car.

My father gave me a brief kiss, let me take his briefcase and the afternoon newspapers. He sat next to Tony and reviewed the day's accomplishments. "Get the lawn cut? Hay arrive? Good, good."

After he had soaked in his bath and changed his clothes and prepared his martini, he perked up and sometimes played pepper with me out under the apple trees. I dreaded these games. He could control the ball beautifully; and as the game progressed he hit it harder, directing the ball at my feet, my stomach and my head. It sent shock waves through my fingers and wrists and arms. And while I had grown adept at fielding it, I felt he was trying to obliterate the ball by driving it *through* me. Even when he was pleased with my performance, even when he described to my mother how well I had done, I was left with a residuum of loathing, a little swollen place inside me that was like a bruise.

After dinner my mother and father began to argue. These were not bloodthirsty affairs—there wasn't as much violence in their voices as in the single whiplash swing of my father's bat. I have heard other voices like theirs since—couples at cocktail parties, even men in an office—two people going along pretty smoothly for a while and then a nerve is touched. The other side puts up a wall, doesn't want the damage seen and so jabs—another ripple of fear; the gentle combat escalates. In the summertime, when the windows were open, my mother's and father's voices came up to my room—never really loud, but harsh and bitter. My father insisted that my mother was forgetful, careless, extravagant. She had been buying a few small drawings and paintings: a Gauguin lithograph, a Marin watercolor, a Mary Cassatt oil of a young woman seated at a piano. These were small treasures and later turned out to have cost a song. But to my father, who did not care about such things, the purchases were evidence only of infuriating prodigality.

My mother in these arguments was a little like me in the pepper games. At first she fielded his anger quite adroitly. But this game went on longer, and as he kept after her, she began to fight back, to complain about his obsession with his work, his materialism, his lack of taste. She called him Stim's "flunky." He grew more testy, claiming that Arthur was at the bottom of their troubles, Arthur was "such a little snob." "You do so love to call him names, don't you?" she said archly —and I could see the coy smile on her face.

My mother and I were jittery, defensive, always a little afraid—afraid of all the rules he had established and of his readiness to "call" us when there was an infraction. It took me a long time to understand that it was not our fear that filled the air, it was *his*; it was the fear of a troubled man who needed to create an elaborate design—it was called "order" —to cover the turmoil that raged inside him, that threatened to break out like a grass fire and destroy all that he had tried so painstakingly to build. To a small boy who feared he might find himself at any moment on the brink of disgrace, the sound of their voices was bewildering. They were playing by an entirely different set of rules. Or perhaps by no rules at all. As I listened to the small brutalities they kept inflicting on each other, I could not help but feel they were also inflicting them on me.

18

AS THE BEECHES spread their branches over glowing beds of myrtle, as cold frames and paths and arbors brought order to the once-ragged landscape, Apple Tree Farm became a jewel—

a small gem embedded in the magnificent setting of Stim's Excelsior.

We were surrounded by four hundred acres of rolling countryside, a dappled landscape of woods and pastures, bridle paths and gleaming white wooden fences—and there were teams of workmen to keep the place exactly the way Stim wanted it. These men clipped the fleece of several hundred sheep and shod the dozen or so horses. Standing on high scaffolding, they pruned the giant maple trees that enclosed the vast rectangular lawn—the Great Lawn, it was called—trimming them squarely as blocks of green stone. Inside, under the high branches, there were cool and dark avenues, still and damp and awesome as the naves of great cathedrals.

On Saturday evenings my mother and father went to Stim's for dinner. Whenever I was invited—Stim considered it a lark sometimes to have his small godson at the table with the adults—the three of us would start out together through our apple orchard on a summer evening, my mother in a longish silk dress and a string of pearls, my father in white flannels and a dark-blue blazer. My mother complained bitterly about these weekly dinner parties, but when she and my father had finished primping before their full-length mirrors, when they were finally on their way, holding my hands as I swung along between them, they seemed content, as though the prospect of good food and drink, gracious service, and the company of neighbors and friends provided a reprieve from their own lonely battles.

After the apple orchard came the silky carpeting of the pine woods; then a rutted bridle path; and then a flat place at the edge of the woods where Stim had placed his tennis court. There would at that hour be two or three men sweeping the court with long-handled straw brooms, others applying lime that shone as brightly as streaks of moonlight on water. My father and mother murmured greetings to the men. "Evening, Brady." "Evening, sir; lovely evening, ma'am." My mother would slip off her high-heeled shoes and carry them with her beaded purse as we moved light-footedly across the soft clay of the court. We went under the arch of the maples and onto the enormous rectangular lawn. The lights were already on in Stim's house at the far end of this vast space, and the dark clumps of box were like guardhouses against its walls.

I loved that house—loved its stained timbered supports, its crenelated towers, its chimneys rising at irregular intervals like steamer funnels—and it dismayed me to hear my mother call it a "hideous old fake."

"Fake?" I blurted out. "Fake *what*?"

"Fake Tudor. It's a copy—a clumsy one—of a kind of house in England that was fashionable during the times of the Tudor kings."

"Hardly think . . ." my father began to protest.

"Of course, our house is fake Georgian. But ours is a beautiful fake."

"Fake isn't the word," said my father. "It's an adaptation."

They began to argue about it, my mother insisting that the old New England houses were the only real ones. I wondered if all the objects that held such potent charm for me inside Stim's house were fake too. The Tiffany lamp throwing scraps of colored light on the green billiard table? The chair in the front hall that had a drawer under the seat large enough for a small child to hide in? The library ladder that slid sideways on a metal groove, like the ladder in Almond's grocery store in Clarkstown? There was nothing remotely like these things at home. And up in Stim's bedroom—kept under lock and key when he was away—were glass cases filled with blue-and-white vases. His Mings, he called them, and he would lie in bed in the morning with his breakfast tray, staring heavy-liddedly at them as though he were half asleep and still dreaming of China. Sometimes I would lie next to him and he would tell me, as he had told my mother long ago when she had first come to Excelsior, how he had gone out to Peking after his graduation from Cambridge to buy up all manner of beautiful objects—Chinese bronzes and Sung landscapes and his beloved vases. Oh, he wasn't supposed to. He was a "great rascal," slipping officials "little tips" to help pack up the booty and arrange for it to be shipped secretly by railroad to the port of Tientsin. Stim's eyes lit up when he told these stories—he was in love with what he called his "skullduggery." It was one of the things I adored about him—he was the only grown-up I knew who boasted about breaking the rules. Only the trouble was, this time, that he had been caught. The old empress rose up in a fury and sent wild bands to attack the big-eared, long-nosed barbarians. Into a sleepy Chinese village where Stim and his accomplices were loading crates of precious goods onto a train came a small troop of horsemen, pigtails flying, and they shot Stim five times in the leg. "Hurt like bloody hell, old man. I toppled forward; I remember a mouthful of dust." And in the Peking missionary hospital they amputated his leg. "You would have been proud of your godfather. No anesthesia, just an old rag to bite on and a bottle of Chinese brandy."

These heady adventures permeated the atmosphere of his bedroom; they made Stim more magnificent and the glowing vases more beautiful. Once when Joseph had just left the room, Stim confided, "You know Joseph isn't his real name at all." And when I expressed amazement, he told me that the major-domos in his father's and grandfather's houses had for generations been called Joseph. Whenever they appointed a young man to the position, they changed his name, and this Joseph's real name was Ambrose—Ambrose Kelly. Only I must never tell. He and I were the only two who knew, except Joseph himself, of course, and probably he had forgotten, although when it had happened, many, many years ago, he had been quite hurt.

Two kinds of guests were likely to be present at Stim's parties, and ordinarily they were not entertained together.

But on a particular summer evening my mother and father and I, walking from the Great Lawn around the corner of Stim's house, saw that both of them were gathered, glasses in hand, on Stim's flagstone terrace.

One group consisted of the neighboring gentry whose vast sprawling houses and stables we saw when we went out riding. My mother had known most of them from the time she had come here on her honeymoon, and if any of them had changed in a single respect, she was hard put to think how. The wives still wore their demure dresses with smallish red-and-blue patterns sprinkled across dark blue shantung. It was, she told my Aunt Agatha, as if they were covered all over with their husbands' neckties. They were always hiring interior decorators to redo their houses. "Poor things, it never occurs to them to do it themselves. No, that would be too daring—too revealing. Do you know, Aggie, that Mrs. Iverson has yellow dahlias on her chairs and her sofas and curtains? But why not dahlia wallpaper and dahlia carpeting and a dahlia dress, so she could disappear completely, like a chameleon?"

And the husbands? Their bright plaid waistcoats, their florid cheeks, their hearty laughter could not begin to conceal their deeply conservative tempers. There were no robber barons here, no men engaged in the running of factories or railroads. Almost without exception they worked on Wall Street, not as financiers starting or building new enterprises but as husbanders of fortunes made a generation ago. Strict education, careful advice, an elaborate mosaic of trust funds had enabled them to preserve their capital through the Depression—indeed, it would have been difficult to tell from looks or bearing or conversation the extent to which they were aware of this cataclysmic event. They kept horses—some for racing, some for the hunt, some for polo; they moored their yachts at Seawanhaka; they owned houses in town and vacationed at Aiken, and in their everyday comings and goings they were sheltered by chauffeurs, by club cars, by lawyers and accountants and a host of servants and go-betweens. They hated Franklin Roosevelt. They hated the thought of another war. They hated the Irish and the Italians and Negroes and Jews. They went to their lovely rural Episcopal churches each Sunday morning and prayed for God's blessings, bellowing their hymns as if still making merry in their undergraduate drinking clubs.

But in the end what disturbed my mother most was the effect their riches had on my father. He coveted not only the physical splendor of their estates, but the thousands of shares in copper mines and steel mills and utility companies that generated a flow of income that was to him like a shower of gold from on high. "Do you know what it means," he would ask, "when Standard Oil goes up a point? It means that Harold Ogden has made another quarter of a million dollars. Think of it!" My mother tried to assuage his envy, "Henry, do you realize how dull they are, how *conventional*?" But it would have the opposite effect—it would confirm his feeling that she was patronizing them. And by what right? He tried to control his temper. "But Sarah, so are *we*. We're conventional as hell." He couldn't have cared less about being conventional so long as he could be rich. My mother, who felt quite differently and who sustained herself in these moments with dreams of her former Starcliffe glory, would say, "We're *not*" (meaning, "Perhaps you are, *I'm* not").

One day, reading an article on atoms in the Sunday *Times*, she looked up with an expression of sly amusement and said, "Neutrons. That's what they are." "Who?" asked my father, otherwise preoccupied. "Our neighbors. They're *there*, no one can quarrel with that. They have bulk. They're probably necessary, although no one can tell exactly why. But they have no *charge*."

It was a tribute to my godfather's social daring—or perhaps his culinary largesse—that on this particular night he was able to commingle the first group with the second. For these others were a different breed: dark-suited, heavyset men who left their wives at home. As the war approached, a greater number of them came from abroad, from places like Bremen and Rotterdam and Marseilles. They would greet Stim with a kind of gruff sputtering effusiveness and then huddle in small groups from which came the strong aroma of cologne and cigars. Their talk was not of yachts and horses, but of coal and cargo ships, of diamonds and turbines. Sometimes Stim produced a more flamboyant character—a designer from Switzerland, a young architect from the city—and while these individuals were more humorous and quick-witted, they were still very much a part of the group, for its coherence came not so much from appearance and style as from its members' shared qualities of alertness and sharp observation. Like electrons, they moved and they were certainly charged, and my mother would have said the charge was distinctly negative. She disapproved of them. She commented that her brother Arthur would never have permitted such people in his house. "For God's sake," cried my father in exasperation, "what does *he* have to do with it?" And when she did not reply, he groaned and said, "Sarah, for the life of me I can't figure out what it is you want."

That evening at Stim's they were all mixed up together on his terrace, talking softly, drinking, smoking and looking each other over. When I shook the hands of the gentry, they assumed a mock-serious pose, as though I were a little adult. The others were more tactile and affectionate; they ruffled my hair, touched me on the shoulders or the chin; sometimes they reached into their pockets for mints or Life Savers or small change. They took me for what I was: a child. To be a child was not only acceptable, it was to have a margin for error.

Stim was splendidly dressed in a maroon smoking jacket and pearl cummerbund. He kept looking at his watch and moving about restlessly until Joseph announced from the door of the house:

"The Count and Countess Lindenskjold."

Stim, smiling, moved toward them.

"Ah, at last!"

Tall, erect, the Count was dressed in beautifully tailored formal clothes, a small pink rose in his lapel. It was not until he shook our hands that I saw how old he was. The flesh had fallen from his broad cheekbones, and the stiffness of his walk had less to do with dignity than with a brittleness in his limbs that he was making an effort to hide.

And the woman whose arm steadied him? Who looked lovingly at him? She was beautiful and young, a willowy, bare-armed creature with fine-spun blond hair, her cheekbones high, her eyes like olive pools. She gave off a wonderful aura of contentedness, and I could hardly take my eyes from her face. But I had never seen a pregnant woman before, and so my gaze kept dropping to her remarkable stomach—it was like a protruding ball, her silver dress pulled across it, the hem riding up a little in front.

"Maude, you are ravishing."

"Motherhood is agreeing with me, Stim dear."

"And Henrik, it's wonderful to see you looking so well."

"So lovely to be here, Stim."

Stim introduced them formally to the guests. When they came to us the Countess exclaimed, "Why, what are you staring at, little boy?"

I was twice shamed. I had been caught looking at an illicit object (that bulge had no right to be there). And then to be called "little boy." Yet I was reassured by her charming smile and her velvety voice; she had an accent, but it was not at all like the Count's.

"You're looking at my baby. How very nice. Would you like to touch it? Then let me sit for a moment. When I walk, he falls asleep. As soon as I'm still, he kicks. You'll see. You'll feel his feet. Oh, what a funny chair."

"That's one of Noll's chairs," shouted Stim. "Noll, where are you? What about women heavy with child—did you think of that when you designed this contraption?"

Noll came forward, bald, roly-poly, his bright necktie like a placard across his shirt front. His chair, he said, should be very comfortable *"pour la jolie maman, non?"*

The Countess lowered herself into the chair, an orange canvas slung between high iron legs. "Oh, it's marvelous, it's cozy. Henrik, you must try it."

"Not this moment, my darling."

"He's kicking already, the little savage. Now little boy, what's your name?"

"Peter," I said, pugnacious and red-faced as my father, "Peter Kempton."

The nails of her slender fingers were the color of apricots. She took my hand and placed it on her stomach. Through the slippery fabric her skin felt tight as a drum. The surface of the drum rippled.

"Feel it?"

"Yes."

"There. Again."

Barely more than the flutter of a butterfly wing. Again. Again. And I felt a powerful yearning to respond. The Countess was smiling, she had forgotten the others gathered around the sling chair. Still holding my hand firmly on her stomach, still listening with our fingers to the tidal kick of the unborn child, she reached out with her other hand and ran her cool fingers down my face as though searching for another beat there.

Joseph announced dinner.

A table had been set up under an awning by the side of the house. Standing kerosene lamps threw spears of light across glass and silver, caught the edges of women's jewelry and the men's cuff links, sent shadows dancing against the timbered walls. First came the fish course—beautiful silver trout caught by Charles Iverson, one of the neutrons, and sent down on dry ice from the Ausable Club.

Iverson had a face like a swollen plum, eyes embedded in the puffy flesh like pits. He fished and collected old fire engines, arriving for luncheon parties with a great clanging of bells. He was sitting at the far end of the table next to the Countess and my father. He began to argue—he was always bellowing obscenities about Roosevelt—and my father said, "Now, Charlie, he isn't a monster, is he?" The Countess said they certainly didn't think so in Europe. She laughed prettily, and she and my father began to talk in low voices. Sitting next to me, my mother fixed her gaze on them.

I knew little of the affairs of the world that weighed so heavily on the guests that evening. My sister was in Paris that summer on a student program. Whenever my mother and father spoke of her, the subject inexplicably veered off in other directions, their quiet discourse filled with references to Munich and the Anschluss. But on the whole, I was more acutely conscious of a villainy closer to home—of our President's unjust and malicious attacks on Wall Street. I had lately been made more aware of these things by the presence of my Uncle Arthur on the front pages of *The New York Times*. There he was, seated in a crowded hearing room before his congressional inquisitors. According to my mother, Arthur was trying to keep the "politicians" from punishing the people on Wall Street. He was arguing that bankers were honorable men, and the reporters who were covering the story said you could see honor written all over Arthur Starcliffe's face.

The waiters passed the lamb—pink and bloody slices arranged on silver platters. A few days earlier I had hidden in the tall grass and watched the animals slaughtered. I heard their terrified bleating and the soft thud of bobby sticks against delicate skulls.

The wine changed from white to red.

My mother and the Count were talking about Picasso. The neutrons patronized her when she tried to explain what it was about the modern painters that appealed to her. She could see their greatness and they could not; and yet when she tried to elucidate it, you would have thought the failing was hers. But the Count smiled and told her that he and Maude had just purchased a small Matisse. They were planning to hang it in their new house in Washington.

Stim rose, magnificent in his smoking jacket. I thought surely Joseph would blow a fanfare and announce, "Mr. Stimson will now make some splendid remarks." A breeze flapped the scalloped edges of the awning; the shadows from the standing braziers danced more vividly. Stim said a few words of welcome to the Lindenskjolds and then, smiling proudly, said he had special news.

"It is my very great honor to tell you that the Danish government has appointed Henrik Lindenskjold its new ambassador to Washington. Henrik will be presenting his credentials to the President tomorrow." And with this he raised his glass, and the chairs made a scraping noise on the flagstones as everyone rose together and shouted, "Hear! Hear!"—everyone except Charlie Iverson, who stood but did not raise his glass. He had not expected to dine with people who actually consorted with the devil.

Dessert came, and the Count, rapping his knife against his wineglass, got a little unsteadily to his feet. His fingers gripped the tablecloth; he began in a soft voice, thanking his dear friend Stim for this wonderful evening, for the fine food and drink and for bringing good friends together. He and Maude already felt very much at home in their new country. When I thought he was about to raise his glass, he stopped and looked over our heads at the benign countryside that lay spread out beyond the fringe of awning. His eyes came back from a long distance and went round the table, taking us in like an old and weary country doctor wishing to satisfy himself that we were *fit*. And gently, quietly, slowly, he began to tell us about what had been happening in Austria and Czechoslovakia. His voice gathered strength. His eyes moved from face to face, willing us to listen. There were evil forces loose in the world, he said—Hitler and his men—and while they might seem far away from us on a lovely night like this, they did not seem far at all from his countrymen. They were on their very doorsteps. Something must be done. His rawboned fist shook and his voice rang out—sharper, clearer, without sorrow or fear—and it was somehow thrilling. I have never forgotten his voice pleading with us on that summer evening.

"These creatures must be stopped—by you! No one else is plausible. Mr. Chamberlain? Mr. Laval? *You!*"

There were no "hear, hears!" this time. The men scowled and the women looked down at their laps in a deadly silence. What right did this stranger have to lecture them? Some of them had already traveled a long distance to escape these fearful battles. They had come here seeking refuge. And the others had for a long time been building fences that would protect them not only from these far-off wars but from fierce struggles closer to home. His face even more purple than before, Charlie Iverson turned to my father and muttered a few words that made the Countess's chin snap up and her shoulders push back against her chair.

The Count looked us over again. There was no doubt that he found us wanting. In his smile now there were weariness and resignation. He was raising his glass, he was drinking to our friendship—the friendship of all of us gathered around this table and to the long friendship of our two nations: "Maude and I drink to that, dear Stim."

To the amazement of everyone, my father—God bless him—was on his feet, shouting "Bravo!," his face aglow, his glass raised high.

My mother gave a little cry. Iverson's face twisted cruelly, the look of a stupid man who has been betrayed. Then the Countess was on her feet beside my father, radiant. Grudgingly the others were getting up, the chairs scraping once again. You could hear the word "friendship" as the glasses touched. But this was a thin, watery kind of friendship they were toasting. It had nothing to do with what the Count had been talking about. It was not the friendship my father had cried out for; his had been a cry from the heart.

There was an awkward silence. It came as a relief when Joseph announced that liqueurs and coffee would be served in the library for the gentlemen and in the living room for the ladies.

The men went silently into Stim's library. I followed them, taking my father's hand.

19

WHEN MY THOUGHTS return to that evening I try again to capture the defiance on my father's face. Even as a child I was aware that he had done something courageous. It was the first sign I had been given that he was not simply one kind of man. If his audacity at the dinner party was utterly at odds with his fierce desire to please and to *belong*, then it was an honorable inconsistency that had its roots, as did these other cravings, in some unacknowledged part of his past. There was in him an unexpected streak of idealism, of boyish adventuresomeness. Part of the adventure had to do with the quest for material possessions—there is no doubt that he lusted after these. But part also had to do with his Uncle Oliver lying on a field of battle, Theodore Roosevelt's Rough Riders charging by.

There were other occasions when my father's views on the League of Nations, on the need to stop Hitler, even his more tolerant views of our President, came bubbling to the surface. Admittedly this happened after he had had something to drink. But out it would come—this passionate Wilsonian idealism. My mother would take him to task, explaining that Henry was a little "tight," Henry was trying to be "different." It was an odd charge coming from her, for this last quality was one that she cherished most in herself. When it came to her own quirky obsessions—Picasso and Virginia Woolf and that strange duck Krishnamurti—she was seen by all the others, my father included, as "different" too—even perverse. She did not understand that when my father got up and shouted "Bravo" he was giving vent to deeply felt views of the sort she held, only his had to do with politics and hers with art. Ignorant of each other's passions, they were determined, whenever they flared up, to snuff them out. And on this particular occasion the matter was complicated by the presence of the Countess Lindenskjold. My father was smitten with her; even my mother, the most obtuse of women, could see that.

20

EVERY SUNDAY MORNING during the summer of 1940 familiar sounds came from the woods on the far side of our apple orchard—the gentle thwopping of tennis balls, occasional bursts of laughter and applause. In the matches that took place on Stim's court, he and the Countess were often teamed against my mother and father, a dozen or so spectators sitting in the late morning under the scented arbors, grapes slowly ripening and yellow jackets flinging themselves about.

Stim loved to play. Before each match he attached a rubber coaster to the end of his wooden leg to prevent it from digging into the clay surface of the court. Thus equipped, he was remarkably agile. He and the Countess, who hit the ball almost as hard as a man, made a formidable team. My father was a dogged if inelegant player, and if my mother's attention could be engaged—she had a tendency to hang back along the base line—they could put up a strong fight. The points then were fiercely contested and the outcome always in doubt. From time to time Joseph came walking slowly across the Great Lawn, carrying a silver tray with glasses of lemonade.

One such morning Susan and I were playing mumbletypeg by the side of the court. My sister was humoring me. She was nineteen years old and in a sullen mood, flinging the knife down into the grass as though she did not care where it landed or what was going on around her. She was still recovering—or so she would have us believe—from a love affair with a Frenchman she had met in Paris the summer before. She had written from France to tell our parents that she was engaged. Her fiancé was not only French but old—thirty-four years old. My mother was appalled, my father furious and determined that something be done.

He went at once to Stim's, and I tagged along. They sat out on the lawn with their brandy glasses and puffed away on cigars, the fireflies blinking off and on as though Joseph were flipping a switch. "I'm going to get Morgan's to run a check on this frog and find out if we can bring charges. Robbing the cradle, assaulting a minor, violating the Mann Act. . . . Do you think they have a Mann Act in France, Stim?"

"Least likely place in the world, Henry."

Puff, sip. Puff, sip.

"My friends at Warburg," said Stim, "tell me there's no way the Maginot Line can hold. Maybe Monsieur François is looking for a way to the United States. An American bride would help."

A long cable was sent and a stern vice-president from Morgan & Cie took Susan to lunch, presenting her with an ultimatum and a return steamship ticket.

Like a star in a musical film, Susan descended the ship's ramp, parasol in one hand. For a moment I thought she would break into song and the little hearts and arrows from her letters float like musical notes over the crowded pier. Her pale silk dress was covered with tiny lavender flowers that matched the lavender of her parasol. She wore silk stockings and high-heeled shoes. Holding her head high, she said, "Hello, Mother. Hello, Father. Hello, Peter," and to each of us she proffered a slightly rouged cheek. The smell of perfume was new too, and when she leaned over to let me kiss her I immediately noticed the large jewel around her neck. So did my mother, who asked, "Where did you get that exquisite stone?"

"The Baroness gave it to me."

"The Baroness?"

"Baroness Irène d'Alembert."

"Goodness, who's she?"

"She is François's aunt."

"Oh, my!"

"Oui, c'est vrai."

I shouted, "Whee, say vray!"

"And the dress?"

"A gift from François." A dreamy look came over her face. "For the long voyage home."

My father said sharply, "How many bags do you have, Susan?"

"Deux. Une grande et une petite."

I whispered to my mother as we walked toward the street, "What's wrong with Susan?"

"I don't know, darling. I think she's being very French."

I watched Maude throw the ball up for a serve, watched her racket come round in a strong arc. *Thwock.* Her stomach was flat.

"Fifteen all," said Stim, puffing.

"What happened to the baby?" I asked Susan.

"She lost it."

"What do you mean, *lost* it?"

"Not so loud, dummy. It came early, and it was dead."

"But I felt it kick."

"It happens sometimes."

"What did they do with it?"

She explained that the baby had been buried in the small town in North Carolina where Maude had grown up.

"Is she going to have another?"

"The Count's awfully old." When I looked puzzled, she added, "Don't you know anything at all? Hasn't anybody explained anything to you?"

"Shush over there," said my mother from the court.

"I know about it. Randy told me. It feels good."

Susan smirked. "That's right. And when you get older, it gets harder to do."

"I thought it got easier."

"Up to a point. Be quiet now and let's play."

She flung the knife impatiently onto the grass and it struck my finger. Blood spurted out.

"Damn you, Susan!"

"*Now* what?" said my father, a ball winging by him.

The game stopped and they all came over to look while I bled and bawled.

"First ice," said my mother, "and then the doctor. Susan, take my place."

Maude placed her hand on the back of my neck.

"If you are very brave," she said, "I will have a small present for you when you return."

But the Countess was not at Stim's when I returned, and I asked Joseph, who was setting the table in the dining hall, where she had gone.

"What did you do to that finger?"

"Susan cut me. I had five stitches. Where's Maude, Joseph?"

"Is it the Countess Lindenskjold you are inquiring after? If so, she's gone to Washington. The Count is gravely ill."

"Did she leave anything for me?"

"Are you the little Kempton boy?" he teased.

He reached into his pocket and pulled out a small silver dagger. "It's the Countess Lindenskjold's special letter opener. She said I was to give it to you."

"Great."

I cradled it in my good hand. I held it by its tip and pretended to throw it. It flew from my hand and struck the paneling with a little zinging noise.

"Master Peter!"

I went over and pulled it out. There was a tiny nick—no one would notice. "What's wrong with the Count?"

"They say it's a stroke. You're not going to throw that thing again, are you, Master Peter?"

I asked him what a stroke was.

"A stroke is what you're giving me with that blade, sir. The blood gets blocked and you get red in the face and topple over in a swoon. I've seen it once in the kitchen. Mrs. Griscom fell over like that."

"And then what, Joseph?"

"When you wake up you're paralyzed and your speech goes slurry."

"Like Mr. Iverson when he's drunk?"

"I wouldn't want to say about Mr. Iverson."

"Will he die, Joseph?"

"I don't rightly know. The first one leaves you weakened. The second one and you are done for."

"Dead?"

"You bet. Now how many times do I have to tell you, put that thing down!"

21

THE WAR CAME lurching toward me on a bright autumn day in 1941.

Stim was expected for lunch. I saw his horse come moseying into the far end of the pine woods and went careening into the house to tell my father. Susan lay on her back on the living room carpet, listening to "Amapola," eyes closed, arms across her chest. In the pantry my mother was placing zinnias in a cut-glass vase like someone throwing darts slow-motion.

"Where's Father?"

"Out back, cranking the ice cream."

In the kitchen the smell of roast beef assaulted my nostrils; the thick odors of gravy, Yorkshire pudding and roast potatoes lubricated the top of my tongue. Fräulein turned from the stove, brandishing a wooden spoon. She was like a cavewoman with a war club; behind her loomed the black stove with its openings full of flickering blue lights. "*Ach!*" She raised her club in her red paw as though to strike me, and I scurried out onto the back steps. My father crouched on the graveled driveway beside a green bucket filled with ice shavings. Embedded in the shavings was a gleaming metal cylinder, and as he cranked the handle of the bucket, the cylinder turned. The dry ice steamed.

"Father, Uncle Stim is here."

Leaves fell slowly from the maple by the side of the porch. The wind caught them and moved them across the driveway. It caught my father's hair and blew it into little tufts behind his ears. His blue shirt was streaked with patches of sweat. The white detachable collar of the shirt lay on the gravel like a curlicued seashell on a pebbly beach. Standing, he mopped his brow with a handkerchief from the pocket of his yellow flannel trousers.

"Tell Stim to bring his horse out back. Tony will take care of her. And Peter, tell him not to ride over the lawn."

"Yes, Father."

I ran through the house backwards, like a character in a movie that was being rewound. I banged into Fräulein at the kitchen table. *"Dummkopf!"* I banged against walls and doors.

"Peter, what are you doing?" My mother carried a crystal vase into the dining room. She held it high, like the cross I carried as an acolyte at the Episcopal church in Clarkstown before my father decided it was no longer "really necessary" for us to attend.

Through the orchard came Uncle Stim on his mare, his Irish setter Sophie romping alongside. Wilhelmina rocked and creaked and strained at the bit, baring her teeth in a fiendish grin. The apples were red and green, and the grass under the trees was strewn with them, pulpy and fragrant. Wilhelmina grabbed a McIntosh, twisted her head, and with her massive jaw crushed it, the pieces so white they made her teeth look like old piano keys.

"Peter the Great!" barked Stim in his gravelly voice. He

was wearing his usual tweed jacket and a hound's-tooth hat that made me laugh.

"Uncle Stim! Father says to watch out for the lawn!"

Wilhelmina pawed the grass, snorted, jerked her head up and down, her right hoof scooping a divot from the edge of the croquet field. Her tail lifted prettily and extruded grainy turds onto the grass under the apple trees. The smell of manure, horse tackle, rotting cidery apples filled my lungs and made my eyes smart with joy.

"Should I turn the old girl around so she can fertilize your father's precious turf?"

"Oh, yes! Have her dump one in front of the third wicket!"

Uncle Stim maneuvered the reins. Wilhelmina's rump loomed over the edge of the lawn. But it was too late. She had "finished her business" (as Fräulein would say). Sophie investigated the steaming turds heaped in the grass under the trees.

"Come on, climb up," commanded Stim.

I lifted my left foot almost to my chest to find the stirrup. Stim's wooden leg hung against the skirt. He gave me a pull. Off we went, Wilhelmina ambling through the orchard, Stim warding off branches with his arm. We came down a slight incline around the side of the house where the kitchen porch and the garage and three shingled horse stalls made a small courtyard. Tony leaned against one of the stalls, smoking. My father straightened up and put his fist into the small of his back and arched it. His blue shirt tightened across his stomach. He held out his arms and I jumped down into them.

"Hand, Stim?"

"No, thanks, Henry."

Stim swung his peg leg over the side and slid slowly down onto the gravel. The puffy folds of cloth around the knee hid the heavy brace. My father walked Wilhelmina over to Tony, who took the reins and led the horse off. Sophie began to sniff the ice-cream bucket. My father gave her a little nudge with his toe and she bounded up the steps and sat there panting heavily. Stim and my father began talking in hushed tones at the edge of the driveway. "The *Kearney*," I heard Stim say.

"Is that a cruiser?"

"Destroyer. Off the Grand Banks."

"How many went down?"

"Everybody."

My father took a sharp intake of breath. "We should have stopped them before." He ran a hand back through his hair and said in a harsh voice, "You know what I hope, Stim? I hope someday we have the opportunity to kill every goddamned German alive."

"Someday is coming, Henry."

We followed my father into the kitchen, Sophie bounding along with us. Fräulein brandished her club at the panting animal dripping gobs of saliva onto the linoleum floor. My father crossed to the double sink and splashed water on his face and reached for one of the dish towels. "*Nein*, Herr Kempton! *Bitte!*" Fräulein threw her spoon down on the enamel-topped table. With my index finger I glommed cake batter into my mouth from a blue-rimmed mixing bowl. "*Nein*, Peter!" Her rough palm came down on the back of my hand.

Fräulein's transformation from nurse to cook was part of a new order of things. Since I would be going to boarding school the following fall, we would no longer need a governess; but why did it follow that if we did not find something else for Fräulein, she would, in my mother's words, "go to Germany and never come back again"?

Fräulein hated it in the kitchen; and she hated it when my father and I came trooping through. But when she saw Stim, her eyes lit up.

"Aaaaaah, Herr Stimson," she crooned.

"It smells like heaven in here, dear Fräulein. I can hardly

wait to enjoy the fruits of your magnificent labors. Do you suppose, dear woman, you could fetch this famished beast a small bowl of water? It would be so kind."

"*Jawohl*, Herr Stimson."

And Fräulein fetched one of the blue-rimmed mixing bowls and filled it for Sophie, who raised herself on her sliding front legs and slurped water noisily onto the floor.

"Thank you, Fräulein."

"*Bitte schön*, Herr Stimson."

They exchanged a few words in German. My mother said this was one of the reasons Fräulein worshiped him—he always spoke a little German with her. And then, of course, he reminded her of the great landowners where she had grown up in Bavaria; like a village girl, she was impressed with his vast estate and his family home.

In the dining room my mother stood polishing silver at the sideboard. She wore a salmon-colored silk blouse and an orange suede skirt.

"How lovely you look, Sarah dear," said Stim.

He took her by the shoulders and kissed her hard on the cheek. She stiffened and pulled back.

"Oh, Stim." She gave a little gasp. "You've caught me like a hausfrau."

"I don't think I'm likely to confuse you with Fräulein, my dear."

"You've got Fräulein eating out of your hand, Stim."

"But not you, Sarah?"

He arched his eyebrows, twitched his mouth, and gave an indulgent little snort. My mother ignored his question; she put down the gray cloth she had been using to buff the serving spoons.

"Oh, Stim, you're not supposed to know about things like polish. You men are supposed to think it shines by magic."

"I'm the one who buys the polish for Joseph. It's called Bright's. It comes from London."

"Mine comes from the Atlantic and Pacific Tea Company."

"Ay and Pee," said my father in a flat voice.

This use of the full name—the Atlantic and Pacific Tea Company—was the kind of archaism that drove him wild. Why, when they were setting out to play golf together, couldn't she simply say they were going to "the club" or to "Saddle Rock," instead of, "We are going off to the Saddle Rock Golf and Racquet Club"? Wasn't she really making fun of their lives by garnishing the names with her little formalities?

My mother leaned back against the sideboard, gripping the brass handles of one of the drawers. My father and Stim stood nearby, Stim surveying the room—glaring at it, really. Susan's record ground to a stop in the living room, thickening the silence. There was a peculiar tension in the air—as though these three were not friends at all, they were at loggerheads, and the secret of it had to do not with my mother's being caught polishing the silver or her odd, archaic language, but with the room itself. It was very much my mother's room—we sometimes jokingly called it the Starcliffe Room. The straight piece of pink marble over the fireplace was one of the few things that had been rescued from the fire at my grandfather's house. The other furnishings she had scavenged from Orion County antique shops in an effort to reconstruct, out of fragments, part of her childhood world. This was where the round mahogany table and the six Queen Anne chairs had come from; and the Crown Derby china and fiddleheaded silver; and the small silver-and-glass chandelier that I loved, its petals of glass revolving ever so slightly, catching the light and throwing it against the cream-colored walls, flakes of brightness that made the walls look more buttery than they really were.

Stim reached out his cane and pointed at the portrait of my great-grandmother, Lila Randolph, on the wall behind my mother. There was a similar portrait of my great-grandfather, Arthur Randolph, across the room, over the fireplace.

"Still got her up there, I see. Old hyena."

"Oh, Stim, please." My mother's cheeks reddened; she was offended.

"Looks like she's had a dose of salts."

I gave a delighted whoop. The old lady had beady eyes and pruned lips; she wore a frilly bonnet and looked childish and mean-spirited. I was with Stim. I couldn't understand why anyone would want to put a face like that on the wall.

"Can't you see? She's a wonderful old character."

"Poor old sourpuss," said Stim a little more gently.

From the living room came the sound of "Begin the Beguine"; from the kitchen, the wonderful aroma of roast beef. My mother started forward, and we all moved toward the hall.

In the library my father shook the martinis. He slipped a tiny crescent of lemon peel into each glass and poured the liquid out through the fretwork in the neck of the silver shaker.

"Stim?"

"Thank you, Henry."

"Sarah?"

"Lovely, dear."

There was now another silence, but here one was somehow comforted by the rough brown upholstery of the sofa and chairs, the soft beige rug, the pleasant glow of the paneled walls. Over the mantelpiece hung a portrait not of a grim ancestor but of Susan and Randolph and me. My father had commissioned it over my mother's objections. There were portraits of this sort hung in houses all over the North Shore, idealized compositions bathed in a lacquered kind of sunlight. In this one, painted half a dozen years earlier, Susan sat in a Louis XIV chair, holding me in her lap. Randolph leaned over the chair and stared down benignly while I craned my head a bit to look up at him. My mother thought the work outrageously sentimental, and whenever someone complimented her on it she would say, in her most sardonic voice, "Isn't it adorable?"

This room was filled with my father's things. The portrait was clearly his; so were the miniature stainless-steel airplanes on the mantel; they had been presented to him by one of his banking clients. The gold-embossed leatherbound books were his, as were the newer volumes—a single shelf of them—that came each month from his book club. None of them had ever been opened. On several of the tables were stacks of business periodicals. When my father was not reading these, he was constantly straightening them, aligning edges and corners of the various piles so that one could see a diligent hand had been at work.

Stim asked after Randolph, and my mother explained he had been carousing with Harvard friends in the city; if he could bestir himself to catch a train, he might show up for lunch. The sly look on Susan's face told me my mother did not know the truth. Susan and Randolph were thick as thieves. There had been a time when he and I had been allies against her—she had gone off to school, leaving us behind. But now they were both in college. They held themselves differently; they spoke a different kind of language, not yet the language of my mother and father but no longer mine. When they talked to me the inflection of their voices changed; they were talking down, and it filled me with dismay. They were moving off and I was being left behind; this time, alone.

Susan had a secret she was sharing with Randolph and would not share with me. She had another she was keeping from my father—this one I was in on—and when we were sitting at lunch Stim gave the secret away. He asked Susan when her French hounds were arriving. My mother's hand flew to her mouth; Susan put down her fork and looked at my father, who paused in his carving and asked, "What hounds?"

Susan turned on Stim. "Oh, how *could* you?"

Stim put his napkin to his lips and said in his deep voice, "I thought your father knew, Susan."

A certain bright look made me wonder if he hadn't told on purpose, if he hadn't wanted to create a little scene.

"Knew what?" asked my father, still not terribly interested.

The napkins were busy. Stim dabbed his into his glass and then onto the lapel of his jacket, where he had spilled a little soup. My mother rubbed away at a little spot on the table.

"They're not hounds, Father. They're puppies. Poodle puppies."

"They're François's puppies!" I shouted.

"So you're in on it too, are you? So it's François again."

The Susan who sat across the table from me was a more subdued young woman than the one who had gotten off the *Normandie* more than two years before. She wore pink lipstick and a little mascara, but the effect was not in the least showy. Her hair was done in a careful pageboy. She wore a dark-blue sweater and skirt and a string of pearls my mother had given her. Her voice was more like my mother's now, with the same cadences and hesitancies as she began, slowly, to tell us about the d'Alembert château, an elegant stone house set in a beech forest along the Loire. She described the harvesting of grapes and picnics along the river and leisurely meals with uncles and aunts in a dining room hung with tapestries that were like windows opening out on that graceful surrounding countryside.

The d'Alemberts had always bred hunting dogs. The ones François's father liked best were his poodles—his "house dogs," he called them, and after he was killed in the Great War, his sister, the Baroness, decided to continue breeding them as a way of keeping his memory alive.

Each weekend guest was assigned a dog as a companion. The one assigned to Susan was Philip the Seventh. He slept at the foot of her bed, he trotted alongside her horse when she and François went riding through the forest. At dinner he lay absolutely still under the table; she could feel his fur against her ankle.

"François said Philip was uncanny."

"What does *that* mean?" said my father.

"I suppose," said Stim, "it means *uncanine*."

Fräulein came through the swinging door with hot fudge and butterscotch sauce for the ice cream.

"It means he could tell when François was in one of his moods." Susan's voice grew more husky. She struggled to light her cigarette; her hand shaking a little, she snapped the lighter once, twice, and then it caught. She blew a puff of smoke. "He could even tell when to leave us alone. . . ."

My mother and father exchanged dismayed looks. Fräulein, caught up in the story, sat down on the edge of one of the Queen Anne chairs along the wall, dishes in her lap.

The d'Alemberts were preoccupied with the war. Would the Maginot Line hold? What if it did not? Who would go where, what would happen to Great-aunt Marie Claude and Grandmother Louise? What would they do to save the tapestries and the furniture, the paintings and the silver? Sometimes they brought up the possibility of Aunt Henriette, who had a place outside London, but this made them burst out laughing; it would be like parking their things in a doll's house. The only person who was at all sure was the old Baroness. She said the men would go off to the front. The young women would go to Spain and Switzerland. The older women—she meant herself and her two sisters and the servants—would stay right there and look after things, come what may. There was only one thing that worried her: what would become of her dogs?

Susan's voice quavered like a car engine not quite strong enough for the grade. Tears came to her eyes; there were little smudges of mascara at the corners of her lids. I had heard some of this story before, but now there was an element of heartbreak in it that made me want to look anywhere but at my sister. I studied my mean-spirited ancestor on the wall.

François went back to the army only a month after she had returned to America. And then the Germans came. "And, as you know, they . . . captured him."

"*Liebchen*," said Fräulein throatily from her chair against the wall.

Stim's hand reached out and covered Susan's. My mother and father sat with fixed expressions, looking only at each other. Did they not know until then that she felt so deeply? They had treated her love affair as though it were simply an adolescent crush. And they must have assumed they had ended it. But here was François again in my sister's shaking voice, in the tears streaming down her cheeks.

"There isn't much more."

François had written her from the front. It was the last word she had received. "He wrote that his aunt was still at the château, she would protect it—he had no doubt of that—and they had gotten a pair of poodles away; that was all an old uncle could manage crossing the Channel. The dogs were Philip and Fanny. Fanny was Philip's chosen bride." She managed a weak smile. "He was confident they would keep the line going. And he asked me, if the war came badly to England, if it came to that . . ." Her voice faltered, she held her napkin against her eyes. "Could the puppies, could Philip's and Fanny's offspring come to America, to *me*, Father?"

Her tears came in a torrent. Fräulein put the stack of dishes on the floor and was next to her, her arm around her, cooing and crooning.

"Of course the puppies can come," said Stim. "And if your father won't have them, *I* will. They'll be grand company for old Soph, won't they, Peter?"

I thought they would be grand company for *me*, especially since Blue, my old setter, had recently been put away. I had been counting on them; I had been counting the days.

My father coughed and cleared his throat and harrumphed away, explaining why of course the puppies could come to us. "Peter and Tony will build a run. Won't you, Peter?" Did he really care, or was he simply saying these things because Stim had forced his hand?

My mother was staring at Susan as though she had never seen her before, as though her story and her emotions and even the girl herself were strange to her. Then she turned her gaze to my father, caught his eye and held it. Neither of them made a move toward my sister.

"Coffee in the library, Fräulein," said my mother.

"I guess Randolph isn't going to come," said my father, disappointment in his voice.

In the library Stim asked Susan about the poodles. Were they standard or royal? What were their names? How were they getting here? And when she told him they were coming in the next few weeks on the *Victoria*, my father interrupted, "I didn't tell you, Sarah. Stim says the Germans have sunk another ship. The *Kearney*, off the Grand Banks."

"Will it ever end?" There was no real alarm in her voice, only a little thrust of irritation. She gave a quick shake of her head, a gesture she made when she wished to dismiss someone or something from her thoughts.

"End, Sarah?" said Stim. "It hasn't even begun."

My mind reeled forward. Fräulein was coming through the doorway with the coffeepot and the demitasse cups. She moved slowly under this load, Sophie in the hallway behind her. But it was not Sophie or Fräulein who held my attention. Against the dark library walls I saw the conning tower of the Nazi U-boat moving through choppy gray waters. I saw the blond captain peer through his periscope, saw him fix the hull of the liner in the crosspiece of his lens and bark the order: "*Ein, zwei, drei . . .*"—and the torpedo slipped silently out of the side of the hull and slithered through the water, slamming the liner amidships. The puppies were deep in the hold, caged in the dark; they barked and whimpered as the water came flooding in. They were drowning in the dark, and I blurted out in a loud voice, which took everyone by surprise, "I hope we kill every goddamned German alive!" Father's words were mine now. And they gave me joy, until I saw Fräulein staring at me, open-mouthed. She advanced with the tray and stumbled a little on the edge of the rug. She was trying to raise one of her hands to her face—was it to find her balance or to ward off the sting of my words?—and the tray began to go, everything sliding at once, the silver pot with the bamboo handle, the demitasse cups my mother had collected; there was the most awful crash I had ever heard. The tray was down; the coffee made a dark, spreading stain on the rug.

Fräulein was bent over, her hands pressing her apron to her mouth. Sophie slid to a stop behind her and yelped between her legs.

I charged toward her. "Fräulein, I didn't mean it. I didn't! I didn't!"

"Nein, nein!" And she warded me off with a thrashing of arms. *"Gott in Himmel."* She turned and ran. I heard her shoulder strike the pantry door.

My mouth went completely dry. The world I had been living in since Stim and Wilhelmina appeared at the end of the pine woods—that world of pulpy apples on the grass, of roast beef sputtering on Fräulein's stove, of slobbering old Sophie, of my father's frothy martinis and smooth ice cream—where had that world gone? It had been crushed like the apple in the snap of Wilhelmina's jaws. Dry-mouthed and dry-eyed, as though every duct in my body had closed and all the fluids stopped running, I watched Fräulein flee from me and knew she would never love me again.

"How could you?" said my mother.

The smell of coffee coming up from the rug was awful.

"Father said it first."

"I've probably thought and said it a hundred times. But not to Fräulein's face."

Who would protect me, who would hold me now that Fräulein was gone? Where was Randy? Where was he! How could I make the others understand? How could they know what I had seen?

"I couldn't help it. The puppies were going *down.*" My shoulders heaved; the vision of the puppies swimming in the cramped hold came back to me afresh.

"Down?" asked my mother.

"With the boat."

Stim reached out from the sofa and took me by the shoulder. "There, there, old man. The puppies *could* go down, you know. But the *Victoria*'s a sturdy old tub. I've sailed on her half a dozen times. She'll come through—and so will they. Now come sit on my lap and give your old godfather a hug."

When my mother and Susan had finished cleaning up the mess, I was instructed to go out and apologize to Fräulein. I hung back.

"Peter," said my father threateningly.

"Go *on,*" said Susan.

I went in slow motion, touching every surface. I burrowed against the pantry door and swung through. In the kitchen sink the pots and pans were piled high. The door to Fräulein's sitting room was closed. I knocked feebly. I didn't want her to hear.

"Fräulein?"

The door opened, and she towered above me, her face wet and purple and swollen. When she saw me she toppled forward—for a horrible moment I thought she was falling again. She was on her knees, pulling me against her bony chest, against an apron so damp I wondered if it was soaked with tears. She held me so tightly it hurt. But as she rocked me, crooning, *"Liebchen, Liebchen, Liebchen,"* I didn't mind, for I knew it would be all right between us, after all.

In the library my mother and father and Stim were standing in a stiff little row by the sofa, all of them looking toward the fireplace, at Randy, who was there with a lovely girl.

"*There* he is. Come over here, squirt, and meet Caroline."

She fixed me for a moment with dark-blue eyes that were almost violet. And then she stared worshipfully at my brother, holding him by the arm, leaning against him. Was this beautiful girl part of Randy's secret? Even though her brief glance was friendly, I did not want anyone to take him away for good.

"Now that we're all here," said Randy, "I have news."

"What is it, Randolph?" said my mother, a note of alarm in her voice.

"Mother, Father, I want you to know I have enlisted in the Army Air Force. I've been accepted into flight training school in the spring."

I squealed with delight and rushed forward and hurled myself into his arms. No one said a word, and when I quieted down and slid back to the floor and stood next to him, I was aware again of the smell of coffee coming up thickly from the carpet.

"Aren't you all just terribly proud?" said Caroline, in a way that reminded me of my sister's old voice. "Isn't it just wonderful?" And she squeezed his arm and flashed her blond smile.

My mother and father and Stim stood before the sofa. My mother shook her head and studied Randolph and Caroline with that puzzled, distant look she had given my sister a little while before. It was my father who was trying to blink back tears. He said roughly, "Well, now!" but failing to conceal his distress turned at last to Stim, who reached out and hooked his hand inside his elbow and held him upright. It was Stim who kept him from falling back onto the sofa.

22

SUSAN, RANDY AND I went to fetch the puppies on a cold December day. The wind came hard off the Hudson and made us shiver as we stood on the dock next to an ocean liner much like the one that had brought Susan home from France two years before. But this ship looked rusty and uncared for, and the sight of it depressed my sister, as though it were a reminder of François, lost in a prison camp, his family scattered. And the puppies? Who knew what they would be like in relation to her sweet memories?

Burly men in drab jackets stood blowing on their hands and watching the crane swing loaded pallets up out of the hold. The flags in the rigging beat high overhead; small trucks and taxis moved along under the elevated highway.

Two small, whimpering black puppies, that is what I expected—two puppies in elegant black leather carrying cases, the kind of poodles I had seen on the city streets, held at the ends of leather leashes by dolled-up men and women; jaunty, nervous city dogs. "Awful yappers," my father kept warning me, and despite my sister's description, this was the image that had taken hold.

I saw them. They stood absolutely still in a metal cage large enough to hold lions. It came hurtling down toward us out of the gray gloom.

"Look at them dogs," said one of the men on the pier.

When the pallet came to rest, the dogs began to prowl,

sleek, black, restless as panthers. But when the cage door was opened, they lost their nerve. Their clipped, furry bodies wriggling in an ecstasy of fear and anticipation, they crawled toward us. It had all been a front. Susan and I burst out laughing. Before we knew it, they tore off, sniffing at pilings and trash cans and prancing about like circus clowns.

"Francine, Philip! Come!" They came to her. "Sit!" They sat.

On the way home I lay in the back of the station wagon with the two of them sprawled across me. As soon as I patted one, the other was there, pushing against my forearm or cheek, insistent for its share of affection. I was oblivious to the outside world, the city streets, the Queensboro Bridge, the flat avenues of Astoria and Queens. My world was with the puppies in the back of the car. And now that they had arrived, none of the rest of the world mattered.

By the time we reached our driveway, darkness had fallen. We honked the horn, but there was no light at the front door and no one came out to greet us. We let the dogs out, and they went bounding around the place, barking wildly.

Susan shouted, "We're here, we're here! God, aren't they the most glorious creatures? Aren't they, Randy? Aren't they, Peter? Randy, what *is* it?"

"Something's wrong." He went bounding ahead of us up the steps while Susan called the dogs.

"Come here now," she said. "I want you two on your best behavior."

They came at once, and she fastened their leashes.

My mother and father sat in the library, listening to the radio on my father's desk. Fräulein was on the sofa, crying. Startled, Susan dropped the dogs' leashes and they went swarming forward, barking and jumping against my parents. "Get them out of here," ordered my mother. "Susan, how dare you bring them inside!"

Francine squatted, and a pool oozed over the carpet, only

a few feet away from Fräulein's coffee stain. Randolph was straining to hear the voice on the radio.

"Listen," my father said to all of us. "It started a couple of hours ago."

It was then we heard the words that would become so familiar: Pearl Harbor, surprise attack, Japs, zeros, the *Arizona*, the *Oklahoma*.

"I'll be called up now," said my brother.

The puppies lay in front of the fire, huddled close. They had been sent all the way across the ocean in order to flee the war, but they could not really escape. Nor could we. Full of foreboding, I went and lay beside them, seeking whatever comfort they had to give, waiting with the rest of my family for the President to come on the air and tell us what to do.

23

WHAT IS IT I long for when I recall those early years before the outbreak of war? Is it simply a hunger for certain sounds and sights and smells—whirring lawn mowers and poodles bounding through the orchard and the whole dazzling wisteria-drenched house standing there before me on a late spring day? Or is it a vaguer yearning for the whole of one's childhood, as though this were an artifact, a precious but lost jewel, bright, full of magical restorative qualities if only one could grasp it?

Alas, I have come to understand that what I miss most was not there at all: words never spoken, arms never thrown open, and the promise, never fulfilled, of an end to bitter and bewildering quarrels.

My father and Susan went to Washington, where they shared an apartment in Georgetown. The horses were sold, the stables closed, Tony and Renata let go. Only my mother and Fräulein and I remained at Apple Tree Farm that last summer. At first I thought all three of us were fighting a losing battle against nature. Now I know that my mother was on nature's side.

She was in a mood different from any I had ever seen her in before—not happy, exactly (she was never really that), but *relieved*. Was it because my father was no longer there to police our lives? I felt a little of that relief myself. Or was it because the place itself was falling to pieces—was the onrush of vine and creeper a confirmation to her that our lives in this elegant North Shore setting had had from the outset a temporary, perhaps even a bogus, quality?

She had surprised us all the summer before by beginning to draw, inspired, apparently, by the marvelous new cutting garden she had planted in a small clearing below the swimming pool. She would sit on the steps that led down into the garden and study the rampant radiance of the place. It was unlike any other garden at Apple Tree Farm, unlike any other garden I had seen on the North Shore. It seemed literally to burst from the earth, a wild blooming of phlox and daisies and snapdragons and iris interspersed with dozens of wildflowers she had purchased from a roadside nursery in Mercersville. I would find her there sketching in the late afternoons, the garden flaring into late summer splendor—fuchsia and apricot and yellow hues flung across the semicircular enclosure like fire across a meadow. Once I caught her unawares, her face cradled in her hands, rocking gently, as though the strain was too great; she could not capture what she wished. The images were as elusive as life itself.

Now in this summer after the onset of war the whole place was breaking free like her garden. Stim would ride over on Wilhelmina and look disapprovingly at the weeds growing up through the driveway. When he asked my mother if he could send over a couple of his men to help tidy it all up, she answered sharply that he could look after my father's precious croquet field, send someone over to manicure that if he wished. Chagrined and baffled, Stim turned away, not comprehending that she was capable at that moment only of caring for the uncared-for. And her way of reaching out to the bedraggled fields and gardens was to try to fix them—to hold them—on the pages of her pad. There was more than obsession here; there was a kind of rapture, as though she were not the only one reaching out—the landscape was reaching out to her, to hold her in a different kind of embrace.

I spent much time by myself that summer, brooding about the prospect of boarding school in the fall. I was thirteen years old—the same age as Randolph when he had gone to Grover. I felt lost and lonely and found myself returning to idle pastimes from earlier years. I lay under the piano in the living room. I set up my lead soldiers, fondled dice, marbles, favorite stones, finding comfort in inconsequential childhood objects that made the world seem tangible and of workable size. My mother was planning to close up the house and join my father and Susan in Washington. What would it be like to wander alone here like a ghost? My ancestors suddenly fascinated me. What kind of companions would they make if, instead of going off to school, I stayed behind? Everywhere I found new companions—in the small fixtures, in my great-grandparents' harsh faces, and in the living room, where, lying face down, I discovered pale doves and slender peacocks in the crimson weave of our Persian rug. Why had I not noticed these things before?

On Labor Day weekend they all came home, Randolph in a sharply creased gabardine uniform, wings on his lapel, Susan with her hair cut short, wearing a prim suit like the ones Miss Boomer wore. My father did not seem much changed. He wore his end-of-the-day look, the one I knew from the Clarkstown station. Caroline arrived, and she and Randolph went off for walks in the woods. When I asked my mother if they were going to be married, she said, "I'm not privy to their plans."

They all lived in a different world, the world of war; and I was not a participant. I could hang a map on my bedroom wall and stick pins in it to indicate the shifting battlefronts, but this was a child's game. All weekend their urgent talk swirled around me—talk of fallen cities and islands, talk of airplanes and ammunition, of propaganda and politics and procurement. When Randolph complained about the lagging effort in Washington, Susan lashed out at him. "Come off it, Randy. If only you knew. Father's working round the clock."

As if to confirm the distance that now separated me from the others, I was not invited to the dinner party that Stim gave that Saturday night. I followed along behind the rest of the family as they made their way across the Great Lawn, Randolph and Caroline hand in hand, my father and Susan strolling together, and my mother a little off to the side. She had looked forward to their return as much as I, but now that they were here she was tense and irritable. I was unhappy because I had been left out; in her case it was almost the opposite, as though they had disturbed the privacy of her new-found world.

I hid under the low branches of a Norwegian spruce at the far edge of Stim's lawn, spying on them. There they all were on Stim's terrace—my brother, dashing in his uniform; Caroline, her white smile visible even from here; my mother and Susan encircled by Charlie Iverson and the other neutrons; the Countess Lindenskjold in a low-cut ivory dress, with little silver sequins like confetti in her hair. She was with my father. Stim came limping along and took her away. Joseph announced dinner, and they all went into the house. I left my hiding place and went along back home.

All night the puppies moved restlessly at the foot of my bed. Whenever someone came home—my mother first, as usual, then my father and Susan, or was it Randy and Caroline?—the dogs raised their heads, barked once or twice, and subsided into uneasy sleep.

Later they scratched at my door. I went downstairs through the dark house to let them out. They flung themselves across the lawn, under the apple trees, into the woods. Something was there, some woodchuck or skunk; in my pajama bottoms and bare feet, I followed them into the night.

By the time I reached the Great Lawn they were far ahead, tearing in and out of the clipped maples. I was entranced by their frenzied pursuit, enthralled too by the softness and brilliance of the evening, the facade of Stim's house lit up and the trees thrown into shadow. My heart opened to the starry, moonlit night. The others, asleep now, might have their particular worlds, but this was mine. Suddenly the gates of the universe had been thrown open and, even alone in this vastness, surrounded by spreading shadows, I no longer had anything to fear—no bogymen, no monsters lurking in the thickets. The pounding of my heart, the electric tingle of my flesh, the heavy sweetness of the night, even the puppies' dashing madly along—these were part of the same fabric, part of the encompassing embrace.

The dogs veered into the woods where I had hidden earlier and went charging along the narrow, winding path that led to Stim's pool, a marble oval in a small clearing of hemlocks. There were low sounds up ahead. Could this be the creature they were chasing? But they crashed off in a different direction, and as I continued along the path I heard voices.

I stood absolutely still. I had not reckoned on others being out in the darkness. It made my presence somehow perilous; but I was drawn forward anyway. I moved slowly toward the pool, keeping to the edge of the path, and then crawled as quietly as I could through the thick wall of hemlocks.

There was a small bathhouse tucked into the woods at the edge of the clearing. I felt its flaking boards against my arm and lay down next to it, extraordinarily excited, afraid that at any moment the puppies would come bounding back and give me away. Someone was moving in the bathhouse, someone was moving from its low step across the grass. There was the sound of a body hitting the water—a sharp, flat splash. I wriggled forward and peered into the clearing, half of the pool brilliantly illuminated by the moon, the other half almost pitch-black. Two figures. A man and a woman at the far end, the woman's hair floating out behind her, part of it spreading into the swath of light. Whisperings. "Lovely, lovely . . ." Was it Randy and Caroline? A small gristle of anxiety told me they were both naked. My fingers dug into the earth, as though that could calm my agitation. Then the woman said, "I'm getting cold, darling," and I knew who she was.

She swam to the steps and moved halfway out; her hair still had sequins in it, but they were made now of drops of moonlit water—water everywhere, sparkling and dripping like silver from her naked body. She came up onto the lawn, and for a moment, until she reached down for her towel, I thought she was walking straight at me. I wanted to see more, I wanted to see who the other person was, still swimming in the darkness; but I was terrified of being caught. I turned and began running through the woods.

When I reached the Great Lawn and looked up at the stars, I saw the silver beads in the Countess's hair. The embrace in which the world had earlier held me seemed to dissolve; there was only an immense void, the distance more frightening than any I had been aware of before. In the moonlight, the tennis court was a banner laid down. When I reached home the puppies were barking at the door. My mother opened it and they rushed by her, into the house. She said in a startled voice, "Peter, what are you doing out at this hour? Come in this minute."

I went up to bed. From the stairs I saw her still standing in the doorway, looking out into the empty moonlit night.

The next afternoon, the Bachrach man came to take pictures of Randy, Susan and me. It was my father's idea; but when the photographer arrived, my father was in a foul mood. My mother went down the front steps to greet him.

"Mr. Bachrach?"

"Oh, no, madam, I'm not Bachrach. Laverne is my name. Sheldon Laverne." He was a pale, flustered man in a heavy, loose-fitting black suit.

"How do, Mr. Laverne."

She never said, "How do you do," the way other people's mothers did. It was a source of embarrassment to me. She swept away up the steps, leaving Mr. Laverne to my father. "What a funny little man," she said. "You won't have to look at the birdie, Peter. Just look at him."

The photographer set up his tripod on the back lawn. Randolph had driven Caroline to the station after lunch, and now he and Susan and I chased one another under the apple trees. Randy whispered to Susan, "What did he say his name was? Lavoris?"

Susan giggled. "Ssssh. Laverne, stupid."

Randy reached for a couple of small green apples and lobbed them onto the slate roof of the house.

"Stop that, Randolph," ordered my father. "They'll clog the gutters."

"Yes, sir." He winked at me.

My mother came out the screen door and walked slowly

along the side of the house. In one hand she carried a gardening basket filled with her drawing materials; with the other she stroked the coarse brick wall.

"How do, Mr. Bachrach?" said Susan, shaking hands with Randy under the apple trees.

"Lavoris is the name," said Randy.

"Full of mouthwash, aren't you?" said I, giggling hysterically.

My brother and sister had decided to have one final taste of childhood, and so they had been miraculously returned to me. We rammed in and out of the trees, from shadows to dazzling light, hurling apples at one another and then coming out onto the lawn, where Randy wrestled me to the ground and sat on me.

"Don't get him mussed up," said Susan.

"He's a mess already. Aren't you, squirt?"

I studied Randy's beard. It had changed; it spread evenly across cheeks and jaw and was coarser than before. For a moment I thought he would do his Jack-the-Ripper act, putting his hands around my neck and making disgusting noises and launching a long foamy dribble of spittle in the direction of my face. But he just sat quietly, lost somewhere, and over his head, past his blue eyes and close-cropped blond hair, I saw fat clouds go by. I was conscious of the earth's turning.

"All right, now," shouted my father. "We haven't all day. Pay attention, you hoodlums."

He shook his riding crop at us. His maroon jersey had come loose from his jodhpurs. He ran his big-knuckled hands through his coarse sandy hair and took a handkerchief from the pocket of his jodhpurs and wiped his flushed cheeks.

My mother sat in the shade of the house with her back against the red brick. Fräulein stood next to her, in a shiny black uniform.

"Father's really getting fat," said Susan with a sharp intake of breath.

"Of course he is," said my brother. "He sits on his ass all day."

"Oh, Randolph," chided Susan, "why are you so *hard*?"

"All right, now." It was my mother's voice this time. She stood and clapped her hands. The sound was like the noise my father's riding crop made against his horse's flank; it broke through the surface of the smoldering September afternoon and brought the world up short: stopped it, put it in its place.

"Your father is being very patient, and so is Mr. Laverne. Please assemble yourselves as you're told."

She stood very straight. Fräulein's stringy gray hair seemed to have melted in the heat; it clung to her skull like a ridged bathing cap.

As we arranged ourselves in front of a low branch, Susan said, "Peter, you've got B.O."

"It's this frigging costume." I was wearing a dark-blue jacket and short flannel trousers. The pants dug into my crotch.

"And straighten your tie; it's all the way over by your ear."

"You're all too lined up there," said my father.

Randy hiked me up onto the branch. I sat with my feet hooked under it, my brother and sister on either side, Randy in a long-sleeved white shirt, open at the collar, and yellowed flannel trousers. In the picture he is tall and lean and the expression on his face is startlingly grave. Susan wears a white summer frock; at the last minute, as I retrieve my gray flannel beanie from the grass and am hiked back up onto the branch, she picks up a wide-brimmed straw hat and holds it. I do not look at the birdie. There is no birdie, only Mr. Lavoris, who keeps saying, "Cheese, children, cheese." My father glowers at us; my mother is in the shadows, quiet, intent, watching. Mr. Laverne's hard-won moment of silence—that instant before his finger presses the slender plunger at the end of his shoelace-cord, an interval charged with the possibility of fixing time *just so*, forever—is broken by the ragged, almost comical sputtering of a small airplane moving across the vast sky. We are still, only I am looking at the plane, not at the lens of the camera, and he implores, "No, look *here*. Cheese!" And Randy, under his breath, advises, "Don't say cheese, squirt, say shee-it." And I break up; in this picture I have a maniacal grin.

Mr. Laverne spent a long time draping us against the limbs of various trees, my father shouting directions and my mother silent—as though she had the picture *she* wanted—and Fräulein down on her hands and knees, searching for four-leaf clovers to bring us luck.

At last it was over.

In a cool, clear voice my mother asked if Mr. Laverne would like a glass of iced tea. It was what my father called her polite voice. Mr. Laverne wiped his brow with a damp handkerchief. Yes, he said, he would very much like some iced tea. And so we sat on the cool covered stone porch looking out through brick archways at the maple trees that provided shade for that end of the house. Fräulein brought the iced tea in a curved stoneware pitcher and poured it into fluted blue glasses. She stuck hollow-stemmed silver spoons into the glasses and added sprigs of mint. Mr. Laverne took a deep gulp and sighed with pleasure. I began blowing through my spoon, making a bubbling noise.

"Stop that, Peter," said my mother.

Randy began blowing through his, ever so softly, caught a look from my mother and stopped. Fräulein passed around butter cookies.

"Such beautiful children," said Mr. Laverne quietly.

My mother asked him if he had children of his own. A look of dismay crossed his face. Yes, he said, they were almost grown up. "And are they in school?" "Aaaah"—it was a funny sound, more like a groan than a sigh—no, they were far away, in Europe. Fräulein, pouring more tea, suddenly straightened up. "Whose side are they on?" asked Susan, almost like my father in her severity.

Fräulein glared at Susan.

"Aaaaaah . . ." He took another swallow of tea. They were on no side; they were *lost*.

Chairs scraped against the concrete floor of the porch. Randy picked up the tripod, and he and my father accompanied the photographer to his car.

My father was in better spirits when he returned. "Time for a swim, boys."

"What about us girls?" said Susan.

"Finally got rid of the fellow." My father took a glass back from Fräulein and drained it.

"I thought he was sweet," said Susan.

"What an odd name," said my mother. "Laverne. What nationality is that?"

"Ah, madam," said Fräulein, "it's *Levine*. Levine is the man's true name. Chewish."

"Oh," said my mother softly.

"What difference does it make?" I asked. "I thought he was creepy." Laverne, Lavoris, Levine—who cared what his name was? They began talking about the war, my father saying something about "all these refugees" and my mother shushing him. I felt the world slipping away from me again. None of that was real, was it? *I* was real, couldn't they see? My heart beat with a sudden strange anger.

"Come on, squirt," said Randy, "I'll race you to the pool."

I was running through the shade of the maples toward the glowing light of the pool. I was tearing at my jacket, dropping it on the ground as I went. "Last one in!" Randy was behind me, gaining on me, dropping clothes too. I came out into the sunlight, full speed ahead, my hands working at the buttons of my fly. My trousers fell, tripped me; Randy would pass me now in a flash. But he reached down and picked me up, hardly breaking stride. We were both naked. He held me close; I could feel his shoulders, slippery with sweat; his beard brushed roughly against my forearm. He ran with me, and took a great leap off the border of the pool and we were flying, flying through the air. He gave a great shout, like a war whoop, and we plunged into the brilliant blue water. It covered us, enfolded us, shut out the world—except for the crazy bright light that danced down through it. A moment or two later we came up, sputtering. Father and Mother and Susan and Fräulein were moving out of the shade of the maples; slowly they came down the grassy slope to the edge of the pool.

24

ON THE DAY of my departure for the Grover School I took the puppies to be boarded in a corner of Stim's stable under Slater's watchful eye. Then my mother and I drove Fräulein to the train. She would join the family in Washington, and I would see her there over Thanksgiving. But the fierceness of her embrace, the tears that streamed down over my face with the specks of cinder from the train made me feel as though our parting would last longer than that.

My mother hardly spoke as we drove north along the familiar roads. Her thoughts were with my dying grandmother, whom she would visit up the valley after she had dropped me off at Grover. And my own thoughts were in a state of turmoil. I had never been away from home before; in addition, I would now bear on my shoulders the burden called Family

Honor. This my brother had manfully upheld in the classrooms and on the playing fields of the school; any intellectual or physical or moral lapse on my part carried with it the consequence of intolerable shame.

When we turned onto Shadow Mountain Road, my mother informed me in an uncharacteristically breathless voice that she had decided not to join Susan and my father in Washington that fall. She had found a small apartment in New York and she was going to study at the Art Students' League. My father and Susan were busy with their war jobs; they would not have time for her. They wouldn't miss her in the least. She gave a little burst of laughter, and I realized that my first surge of apprehension had been misplaced; this decision of hers was simply another of the new arrangements dictated by the war. My hopes rose wildly at the possibility that I could stay with her in New York and go to school there, instead of Grover, only a few miles ahead of us on the road. When I suggested this, my excitement mounting, she told me the apartment was "tiny." I said I wouldn't mind; but oh, how firm she was. What about Fräulein? I asked, what would happen to her in this new scheme of things?

"We've said goodbye to Fräulein."

"We have?" I was aghast.

Fräulein had a job with a family in New Jersey. "Nursing a newborn babe. . . . I thought it would be easier if you knew afterward."

"No!" I shouted, "no!" I hit the window as hard as I could with my fist.

When we reached the school in the late afternoon, I saw the words "Fortitude Compassion Truth" inscribed on the marble arch of the gate. My courage, my expectations, my very soul—these were shrunken and enfeebled things. In the distance, beyond the green playing fields, in the shadows of the thickly wooded hills, stood a row of Gothic buildings—squarish, dimly lit structures with small windows and gray facades. I heard the tolling of bells, which would summon us to morning chapel, to classes, to meals, to athletic events, to evening study hall. If you were off across the valley the tones were rich and soft and beautiful, but up close, with echoes coming back from the nearby hills, they swam together, eerie and heavy and dismal.

Each morning the alarm went off at six-thirty on the top floor of Jefferson Hall. Each morning I reached for my damp towel and plodded down the dark hallway to the bathroom, where a dozen or so of us gathered under bare bulbs that dimly illuminated dark concrete walls and washbasins caked with soap and hair. Other boys sat straining away on the toilets, the open stalls barely visible in the steaming mirrors over the sinks. The room stank of armpits, piss, stools, oily hair lotions. Outdoors, unfortunate comrades worked off demerits by running laps in the early morning chill.

In the vast paneled chamber of the dining hall, in the chalk-scented classrooms, in sulfurous laboratories and in the chlorinated, green-tiled swimming pool, it was as though there should be one more light switch to click on, one final burst of electricity or gunfire required to dazzle or obliterate these various places. As one's eyes gradually grew accustomed to their dimness, the bells would ring out, thickening the gloom.

Wandering through our house that last summer I had imagined staying behind and haunting the shuttered rooms with my ancestors. Now I became a ghost at Grover instead, a dogged but solitary figure lurking at the edges of groups or sitting silently at the rear of classrooms. There were other family specters here: Uncle Arthur's pink-cheeked face stared down solemnly from the rotunda in the Starcliffe Library; Uncle Flint's name was emblazoned on brass plaques commemorating winners of golf and tennis tournaments held before the First World War. And my brother Randolph was everywhere present, his name inscribed on trophies, his firm handwriting coming up to greet me on library cards pulled from manila pockets in the backs of books. When I ran my fingers over those smooth, stiff cards, it was almost as though I could touch him. And he was present in the eyes of various masters, who recalled his feats on the football field and the track. They asked after him; they sized me up. But to emulate Randolph would have been a kind of sacrilege. One did not compete with beloved heroes, one worshiped them. Certain of this course, I drew deeper into myself, did my work as dutifully as before but as silently as possible, volunteering nothing.

Each month I received a formal note from my father, enclosing my allowance. He would ask a question or two about my studies; he would comment cautiously about the war and then sign off, "Love, Father," his full name typed below, his secretary apparently wishing to remind me who he was. My mother sent an occasional postcard written on the run: "Drawing going well"; "Aggie and I doing the galleries"; "Susan here briefly." From the vast playing fields along the side of Shadow Mountain Road I thought I saw her car go by. Three or four times I looked up from a game and was sure I caught a glimpse of her, a scarf over her brown hair, her gloved hands on the wheel. If she was going to visit my grandmother, why didn't she stop to see me?

Then my grandmother finally died. When she had become seriously ill in the early summer, my mother stopped taking me on her trips to Ellsworth Falls. And so as I stood at her graveside with the rest of the family and Dr. Willoughby and a dozen or so others from the town, I had the strangest feeling that she had died a long time before.

"You've got it all wrong, bloody idiot," whispered the strange boy sitting next to me in study hall. His slender nail-bitten fingers scribbled furiously; he shoved his version of the equation in my direction. I began to ask him who he thought he was.

"Put the *x*'s over on the left. You'll see."

He was right; suddenly I saw.

We walked back to Jefferson together in the gathering winter dusk. He was a slight boy with fair hair that drooped across a pale forehead, and a skinny neck that rose from his shoulders like the stem of a flower from curving leaves. Kenneth Almyer Andrews was his name, but for years I called him Andrews. He came from Scotland, one of a handful of boys from the British Isles who had been sent to Grover for the duration of the war. Our headmaster, a bullet-faced man named John Nicholson, had made a plea on behalf of these special newcomers in his opening address to the school, an oration in which German submarines were used as a metaphor for our own lurking cowardices. On and on he went, his voice rising to a kind of blubbering frenzy as he exhorted us to shun the Sneak Attack and to vouchsafe that our visitors would find no occasion to describe this land or this school as an inhospitable place. "Gentlemen, we are fighting a war here, each of us, against our secret and lesser selves. I expect us, with God's help, to *win* that war. Now let us pray."

Warily I entered Andrews' dark ground-floor room. I was confronted with an amazing clutter of rocks, birds' eggs, butterflies, dried grasses and vials of brightly colored powders. The contrast with my own tidy abode could not have been more striking.

"I'm trying to figure out whether to be a botanist or a chemist."

I was flabbergasted at the notion that one could consider what to "be."

"Tea?"

"Here?"

He pulled a small Bunsen burner from beneath his bed and began to pump it. "Open the window, will you? This stinks like bloody hell."

"Are you allowed to have that thing?"

"Of course not, but one can't drink that swill in the dining hall."

He pulled chipped china cups and saucers from under the bed, and before long we were sitting on the floor sipping Twining's Orange Pekoe Blend, and in his pleasant, purring voice he explained that his father, Lord Lochaber, was serving with General Montgomery in North Africa. He took a photograph from his desk and showed me a vigorous, mustachioed man standing in a kilt on the steps of a magnificent stone castle. There was another framed photograph on the desk, of a scowling, bearded man in a soft, wide-brimmed hat; this, I was informed, was Darwin. When I said I didn't know who Darwin was, Andrews explained that he was one of the greatest men who had ever lived. That was what his father said. Darwin and Freud. I did not ask about Freud.

On a rare visit, my mother informed me that I had "shot up"; I had "broadened out"; I had "*changed.*" If Andrews resembled a slightly fidgety borzoi, then I was more of a retriever—taut-skinned, muscular, rangy. We must have made an odd pair, tramping over the Orion countryside that first winter. I was astonished at how much my friend knew, and how much of it he had learned from his father. They had hill-climbed and fished over the Scottish Highlands; they had read and traveled together; and all the while the older man had shared with his son an apparently inexhaustible store of information having to do not only with flora and fauna but also with classical mythology and English literature and Newtonian physics. Like my father and Stim and Arthur, Lord

Lochaber was a banker; he had a small office in Edinburgh and was responsible, I was told, for "one of the trusts."

In class Andrews was nearly as quiet as I. It was part of our bond. But when he was called on, he suffered none of my discomfort and shyness, answering questions calmly and authoritatively. When he studied, he shut out the rest of the world; he was lost in his work, and the only movement he made was a slight clenching and unclenching of his fists, as though he were using his fingers to force material into his brain. On his desk he kept a row of small volumes: *The Book of Wildflowers*, the books of *Ferns*, *Minerals*, *Insects*, *Grasses*, *Rushes*, *Butterflies* and *Moths*. These short guides connected him to a domain previously invisible and still largely inexplicable to me. They helped him divide this realm into manageable segments, so he could then grasp it, the way he held a small, fluttering moth in his fist, absorbing the creature into his head: Heterocera, green pea, cream-bordered. "Come over here, Kempton, look at this." He would sit me down before his microscope, and as I adjusted the lens there emerged from the milky blur a bloom of vivid colors. From him I learned many things, wondering all the while what there was for him to learn from me.

When Thanksgiving came I went to New York instead of Washington, and, because my mother's apartment—a small walk-up in the shadow of the rumbling Third Avenue El—was indeed tiny, I stayed with my Uncle Arthur.

I felt a sharp pang of disappointment; I had nurtured the hope that I would be allowed to stay at Excelsior with Stim, but my mother put an end to that desire before I could even begin to express it. Arthur was expecting me; he was looking forward to it; he had a lovely apartment, and it was within walking distance of hers. And so it was decreed, and I went as instructed to the fine building on Fifth Avenue where my Uncle Arthur lived overlooking Central Park, a quiet place so burnished and buffed it appeared no one inhabited it at all.

Everywhere there were gleaming surfaces—long stretches of parquet wood floors and mahogany tables; shot-silk chairs and sofas; thickly varnished paintings of clipper ships and of jockeys astride glowing chestnut thoroughbreds. I have since met other men (I suppose my father was one of them, although his efforts kept unraveling at the seams) who in their passion for tidiness suck the life out of places.

Arthur was sixty years old that winter, the senior partner of Grenfell, Starcliffe and Company, and from his office on the corner of Wall Street and Broadway one had a splendid view over Trinity Church, the harbor, the Statue of Liberty and the low-lying Jersey shore. I did not understand the qualities that accounted for his success; but there was no gainsaying the respect in which he was held by the men in his office, or by the press, which was constantly badgering him for predictions. Nor, when I grew to appreciate these things better, was there any doubt about the quality of the objects with which he had surrounded himself in his Fifth Avenue apartment. The silver was by Revere; the glassware, Waterford; the tall clock in the hallway, William Hill, 1820. The paintings, disparaged by my mother, included a George Inness landscape and a New York street scene by John Sloan. Arthur's taste had nothing whatsoever to do with the new—certainly not with the avant-garde—but his eye was superb. Although the advice of experts was readily available to him, he made these purchases himself, and in these, as in all his other transactions, he was canny and assured.

But the man himself? He might easily have passed for an apothecary or a haberdasher. What would have been vanity in another man—the careful way he brushed his thick, snow-white hair—conveyed in my uncle's case only meticulousness and mildness. Arthur was trim, fresh, alert. He wore dark suits and white shirts and plain dark neckties. His shoes came from Cobb's. They were bought to last, and he polished them himself. His voice was neither soft nor loud, neither deep nor nasal; it was a plain, unassuming, Midwestern kind of voice. It was years before I came to appreciate the gentle way he kept asking questions, not meddling, not doing anything, really, except indicating that he was genuinely interested, he wanted to know.

This was not the Arthur my mother had described on our rides to Ellsworth Falls. This was not the young man who had come home from the Starcliffe Works to hector his father; it was not the same person who had tried to manipulate my father. But of course I did not understand then how time softens some men, coarsens others, and provides still others with a veneer.

At seven-thirty in the morning, the sky darkish, a wind gusting around the corners, we were heading down Fifth Avenue, Arthur explaining which industrialists had built which ornate mansions. We went past the Plaza and the great department stores, past Aggie's store—Birnbaum's, on the corner of Thirty-eighth Street—and gradually it became clear that Arthur intended to walk all the way to his office. His pace never faltered; he waited for the lights to change and stepped off briskly again, all the while giving out little snippets of information. Here there had once stood an old button factory; in a dreadful fire, hundreds of women and children had perished. Where now a golden-domed insurance company housed its employees, there had once been meadowland. Over the years I took these walks with him many times, and from this running commentary my sense of the city changed. It was no longer made up of immutable skyscrapers and streets; it was dynamic, in constant turmoil, although less so, perhaps, in those war years than in the years past or those to come.

The Grenfell, Starcliffe office was a simple, sunny place. My uncle's corner office had a desk bare of papers, a leather sofa, a few framed prints of harbor scenes. There didn't seem to be anything in the room that one could call "work." He asked whether I would like to stay awhile, or if I preferred going back uptown, in which case the IRT subway was on the corner outside the building. When I told him I thought I would visit my Uncle Stim, there was a brief contraction of the flesh at the corner of his eyelids—that was all—and he said, "All right, young man; do you know where it is? Here, I'll show you." And he drew me a little map.

In the dungeonlike anteroom of Stimson and Company, a lamp threw a circle of gold on the timbered ceiling. The elevator creaked down, and Miss Boomer, hands clutching her pince-nez, came toward me. Mr. Stimson was "tied up." "Perhaps another day, dear? Mr. Stimson would very much like to see you over the Christmas holidays. And what do you hear from your father?" She was giving me the brush-off; a nervous woman, fidgeting with her glasses and running her hand quickly back through her gray-streaked hair, cut shorter than I remembered, almost mannish.

I rattled around in Arthur's apartment for most of that long weekend—only rattle is not the proper word, for it was not a rattling kind of place. I sat in the library reading or listening to the radio. Arthur gave me pocket money for sodas at Schrafft's and the movies. When we were together in the evenings, he drank a large bourbon old-fashioned while I had Coca-Cola, and we engaged in sporadic conversation, both of us reading papers or magazines and trying hard to think of things to say. He asked about my studies and school, about Randolph; he spoke a little about the war; he grumbled a bit about the market, in the same way as my father, only with no tension in his voice. I was disappointed that in lieu of my boarding school, I had this lonely place, and for company a man who might just as well be a schoolmaster. Of course, it did not occur to me that Arthur's little formalities and attempts at humor—his calling me "young man" and asking if I wouldn't like another "cocktail"—were the efforts of a man unaccustomed to children, indeed, unaccustomed to much company at all. When I was leaving, he said quietly, helping me on with my coat in the hallway, "I do hope, young man, that just because your father and I . . ."—I do not remember exactly what he said next; it was an excruciatingly awkward moment—"that you and I can be friends."

I did not know how to handle this olive branch, offered at just that moment when our eyes could not meet. In my youth, my ignorance, my embarrassment, I turned, and instead of pecking him on his cheek as I ordinarily would have done, I held out my hand and said, "Thank you very much for the weekend, Uncle Arthur." I did it more out of shyness than unfriendliness. But I could see that he was rebuffed—there was a brief blinking of the eyes behind his rimless glasses. Then he smiled his sweet smile and rang for the elevator, and we stood silently in the foyer with its chinoiserie and gladioli, and when the elevator came he said a little wistfully, "Next time perhaps you would like to bring a friend."

Arthur had met Andrews' father on a business trip to Scotland, many years before. "Do you still have the house on Charlotte Square? Yes? Well, your father invited me to tea there, and I had a most enjoyable time." And he began to give us a little talk about investing. We rolled our eyes at each other, but when Arthur spoke of the grit of the Scottish financiers, I could see Andrews was pleased. "So much shrewder than the Swiss," said Arthur. "The Swiss are really adept only at secrecy. They always think they're about to be invaded, that someone's going to take their bank accounts away. But the Scots!"

Sometimes Andrews joined me at Arthur's, sometimes he stayed at school, foraging the countryside for his specimens. He did not mind remaining up there with only a handful of boys and masters; he preferred it to visiting his mother, who had established herself in southern California with what he scornfully called "her bloody expatriate pals." From time to time she sent him a handsome check, which enabled us—as my meager allowance did not—to engage in an orgy of moviegoing. Now and then we visited my mother's apartment. The place was an incredible jumble—not unlike Andrews' room at school, but without any discernible organizing principle. There were piles of dishes and bowls of decaying fruit; I could not distinguish what she had intended to paint from what she had once planned to eat. She sat hunched over a sketch pad, working away furiously. She barely spoke to us; she hardly noticed we were there.

At Christmas we went to Agatha's, and there, with the lovebirds chattering away in their gilt cage, my mother spread out her drawings on the floor. She was going to let each of us select one as a present. My father, Susan, Aggie and I stared down at the charcoal sketches—nudes and still lifes and the facades of buildings, all of them quirky and contorted. My father puffed his cheeks out and hummed.

"A little like early Kandinsky," said Agatha.

My mother burst out laughing. "Oh, Aggie, come off it."

"Who's Kandinsky?" asked my father.

Peering into the cage of fluttering birds, Andrews remarked, "One of these fellows looks a bit under the weather. Mind if I have a look, Miss Kempton?"

"Agatha to you, young man. Let's take a peek at the poor old thing." She drifted down to that end of the room, and one by one the rest of us chose from among my mother's drawings.

"I must say you don't seem noticeably enthusiastic."

"They're most interesting," said my father.

"You have real talent, Mother," said Susan.

My mother snorted. Praise and lack of praise—both seemed to undermine her confidence. Yet when she saw the drawing I had selected—a still life of apples and peaches against a green cloth drop—she said excitedly, "Oh, Peter, I'm so glad. It's my favorite."

In a burst of Culture, my mother and Aggie took us through the Metropolitan Museum. As we lingered before Impressionist paintings, I could see that Andrews was eager to be outside in the park studying the marine life at the edge of the boating pond. One evening, he and Aggie and I climbed the steep grillwork stairs to the balcony at Carnegie Hall and heard Schnabel play a Mozart concerto. I closed my eyes and listened to the notes float up, mellow spheres like bells—only these were not like the Grover bells, these were plummy and serene, the curving line of music having less to do with the touch of fingers on keys than with the caress of felted hammers on steel. I opened my eyes and saw Aggie smiling, tears on her cheeks. When it was over, we began to clap wildly.

With the spring came light. Now we could see the bone structure of the hills. Across the valley, shorn of its opaque covering, the gentle river bubbled along on its run to the sea.

In the late afternoons I listened to music in the house of the chapel organist, an old German named Kellner. He croaked the various themes in a hoarse voice, attempting to clarify for me the intricacies of the sonata form. The arrival of spring, my long walks with Andrews, my discovery of Beethoven and Brahms and Wagner—these things afflicted me with longing like a fever. I wanted to hold someone. As I grew, the space inside me grew. My heart beat in an enlarged cavern.

Even in this remote valley the war hung over us like a pall. The younger masters were off fighting it, and we were left in the hands of a group of older men whose collective frailty cowed us. Stirring chapel talks by "Sneak Attack" Nicholson reminded us of the peril our loved ones faced, and of their need for our prayers. In the classroom we followed the progress of the Allied forces, comparing this war with ones that had come before. Invested with a kind of instant holiness, El Alamein, Stalingrad and Guadalcanal took their places beside Yorktown, Bull Run and Verdun.

In one's early childhood there is only a vague sensation of individual days falling away in a blur. Now there was a palpable awareness of the passing of seasons, of terms, of vacations with Arthur, of a first year and a second. In this sharpening of our perceptions, the war again played a part. But it had its own peculiar ebb and flow, and under the surface something powerful was building, an irresistible force, a juggernaut.

Andrews received frequent letters from his father—first from North Africa, then Sicily, then Italy, as the tide of the war turned. He read them aloud, and I could see the source of his acute powers of observation, for the letters were full of vivid descriptions of landscapes and villages and people. I envied him the bountifulness of this correspondence, and the ease and warmth with which he replied, for he read me portions of his own letters to make sure he had properly caught the flavor of a particular event. I began a correspondence of my own, not with my father or my mother, but with Randolph. At first his replies were short and breezy and debonair, full of fraternal boasting about booze and girls and the exploits of his B-24. But slowly the letters changed, and the time came when I was no longer sure I knew who my brother was. It made me long to see him all the more; it made me wonder if I had changed too.

It came as a surprise one March afternoon to hear a knock on my door and to find George Budlong, my dorm master, standing in the hallway with a pair of baseball gloves and a ball.

"Come with me, Kempton."

He was the prototypical Grover master, a shaggy, laconic man with a roll of flesh poised over his belt like a lump of dough.

"Let's throw a few."

"Isn't it getting awfully dark, sir?"

"Naw."

We walked down the grassy incline to the varsity baseball diamond. The sun had set behind the low hills and in the lavender afterglow the clay of the pitcher's mound was as livid as raw flesh.

"Mucky down here," said Budlong. He crouched near the backstop, threw me the ball, gave a barrage of instructions about warming up good and slow, easy motion, keeping it low, aiming for the mitt—all this from his crouch, his stomach splendidly rippled under his checked shirt.

I threw my first pitch into the sodden grass in front of him. The ball skipped past his glove, past the backstop, down the bank into the stream.

"Shit."

"I'll get it, sir."

"Good boy."

He wiped the slimy ball across the front of his shirt, leaving a brown stain. "Don't aim the fucking ball, *throw* it."

I threw the ball. It went whirring by his head, striking the backstop. My third pitch hit the ground, bounced up and struck him in the groin, propelling him backward on the wet grass. He sat there, glove over his crotch.

"Are you all right, sir?"

Budlong staggered up, threw me the ball and crouched again. "Throw it! None of that wind-up bullshit."

I threw the ball easily into his mitt.

He threw it back.

Again.

Back and forth we threw. I could hear the stream rushing by, smell the heavy wet earth on the base paths. The ball shone in the violet light; gleaming, it flew back and forth, thudding into our mitts. Budlong began returning it a little harder, with a snap of his wrists. At last he said, "Enough for the first afternoon. Not bad at all, Kempton. How's the old wing?"

"Fine, sir."

"Sloan's liniment before you go to bed."

We walked back up the incline to Jefferson, Budlong placing the weight of his hands on his thighs and pushing himself up the hill.

"Throw a few tomorrow, Kempton?"

I didn't much want to, but I was afraid I would hurt his feelings.

"All right, sir."

"Soak the arm."

The big bells began to toll, their shivering notes cascading down the valley. As Budlong went into his quarters, Andrews came loping out of the woods, a butterfly net under one arm.

25

WE FILED INTO the Lord Chapel one Sunday morning and to our astonishment saw Uncle Arthur sitting in the place reserved for the guest rector. He wore black robes and held a hymnal in his lap and seemed completely at ease.

When the time came, he walked to the pulpit and, with his face barely peering over the top, gave a sermon on the subject of Rebuilding the World. The war would soon be over, and it would be up to the likes of us to help put the pieces of our shattered globe back together. And what qualities would that require? Every boy in the chapel knew. We had been made familiar with the great litany of "selfs": self-discipline, self-control, self-knowledge. There was no need for my uncle to mouth these platitudes yet again. I threw Andrews a desperate look. Arthur was describing the first time he had come to the school, in a horse-drawn buggy. "It was a different era, and yet the same qualities of character were called for." He had passed under the marble arch and read the pieties inscribed there and yes, he had taken them to heart. That was why he was standing up there so confidently, telling us how to lead our lives. Oh, why didn't he sit down and be still? Thank God no one but Andrews knew he was my uncle.

But they knew soon enough, for there was a gathering of masters and seniors on the steps of the chapel, and when he saw me, Arthur exclaimed, "Ah, here's my nephew. And Kenneth, how are you, young man?" He took us to lunch at the Grover Inn, and after he had returned us to Jefferson in his chauffeur-driven limousine one of my classmates smirked, "How is your Uncle God?"

"Come here, you little limey bugger," said Budlong as he and I worked out on yet another twilight afternoon. "Come here and swing this thing." He handed Andrews the bat.

They were trying to draw me out of my shell. Old Kellner had me singing in the glee club; Budlong, now varsity baseball coach, had been grooming me, first on the Jefferson team and then the jayvees, and soon, he said, I would be ready to start "one of the big ones."

Once, high up in the hills, Andrews and I were deciding whether or not to cross an icy pond. If we fell through, no one would know, no one would come to rescue us. It was then he confessed that he had no physical courage. His father had seen this in him and told him it made no difference—some people simply did *not*. They made up for it with other kinds of courage. "Like what?" I asked, a little resentful that cowardice could be acknowledged this way, even condoned. He thought for a long time, but did not answer me. Finally, we did not cross the pond.

As I became more involved in the activities I have described, as I began to shed my translucent skin of ghostliness, my friend seemed to become more reclusive, wandering the hills in an olive jacket that had a multitude of pockets for his treasured objects. His room was more than ever a laboratory. His work was increasingly recognized as brilliant, and as we progressed from term to term he was often excused from regular work to engage in special projects.

Now he stood before me with his bat, a spider of a boy, the bat like the wobbling feeler of a praying mantis. I winged the ball straight down the middle of the plate and saw him cringe and jump back.

The day of my first varsity assignment was balmy and fragrant, a May day in 1945. The sun poked in and out of the clouds. My mood was similarly varied, sharp pinpricks of anxiety charging me with excitement and giving way to lassitude and gloom. Andrews came to my room and comforted me with tea and crackers and droll inquiries about the state of what our headmaster referred to as our "mental equipment," as though this were a helmet one pulled on in times of crisis.

In my fantasies I had played the game a dozen times on the pages of the *Grover Reporter*. The headlines were sharp-edged and explicit: ORION NINE BOMBARDS GROVER ROOKIE; GROVER NINE OBLITERATES GREEN BEHIND ROOKIE STARTER. Both victory and defeat were couched in the language of the day's headlines. Allied forces—Andrews' father among them—were sweeping across Western Europe, inflicting savage blows on the enemy, overwhelming him the way I hoped to overwhelm the Orion batters that afternoon.

Budlong had called my father in Washington to tell him I was making my first varsity start, and to suggest that he might come to the game. My father had not yet come to visit me at school. He was a busy man; lately he had been traveling all over the world in his search for strategic materials for our troops. I did not know whether I wanted him there or not. His presence would rattle me. And yet . . . Pacing the room before the game, I recalled the summer evenings when he had sent his wicked line drives flying toward me. I remembered how the ball had stung, the pain going up my arms. And the memory made me miss him and hate him; in a fury I flung the ball I had been holding across the room. Startled, Andrews looked up. I wanted my father there. I wanted him there so I could pitch to him, throwing the ball at him with all my might. I imagined him raising his hand to ward off the blow —but too late. The ball struck the side of his temple; with a cry he fell, and the spectators came streaming to him from the stands.

My father was not in the bleachers when the game began, but Uncle Flint was. Flint, thin as antimatter, lifted a bony fist and shook it as encouragement. I hardly noticed, I was shaking so hard. The resin bag slipped from my fingers; when I threw my warm-up pitches my limbs were no longer attached to my body.

I walked the first two batters and struck out the next. The clean-up man, a stocky blond boy, waded into a fast ball and creamed it so hard it seemed to flatten during its lofty flight. The outfielders stood with their backs to the plate, hands on their hips, watching. The ball dented the shining hood of one of the parents' cars at the far edge of the field.

Budlong stood beside me on the mound. "Lost your nerve, Kempton?" I stared at the dirt; I did not want to look him or anyone else in the eye. He gave me a little pat on the rear end and walked away.

I gave up two more runs, but the Grover team scored some

runs of its own, and the game was somehow tied in the fourth. I was breathing more normally now. There came a moment in the fifth inning when I stepped off the mound to wipe my face with the back of my glove and saw people sitting happily in the stands, sweaters and jackets folded on the bleacher boards. I saw Andrews peering intently at me; saw Flint smiling, quiet; saw the gleaming cars parked along the road. I began my wind-up, my motion fluid, gentle pumping of the arms, stretch of uniform across the shoulders, foot going up, up, arm back, straight over the shoulder, close to the ear, *release*. The ball sprang for the deep dark pocket of the catcher's glove and rammed there with a thud that surprised him. He threw it back, took his hand out of his glove and blew on it. I studied the pocket of the catcher's glove as intently as Andrews had ever examined a moth. I threw the ball again, so easily I was hardly aware I had done it. When it came back, I examined its seams, felt its smooth horsehide cover. In my delirium the texture and proportion of things seemed marvelously altered.

Budlong came out again. "Easy, kid. Don't forget, we've got nine innings."

"I'm okay." I wished I could pitch and bat too, returning the ball to myself on a smooth, level trajectory, catching it, completing the cycle. That fleeting moment of anguish gave me the only hint that the world was not complete, that everything was not fixed in place.

My teammates came like phantoms and demons, embracing me, lifting me off my feet. In the last five innings I had struck out twelve men. When had we scored the winning run? How could I have been so deeply alive and in so deep a dream? Flint came over, put a skinny arm around me; Budlong smothered me in a hug. The crowd was walking away. Cars were starting up. The players made their way to the gym. I lingered at the edge of the diamond; I wanted to stay a bit longer. Andrews and I sat together on the bleachers. As I rested, the world came flooding back—fields and trees, chunky Gothic buildings already in the shade of the hills. Clouds covered the sky; it felt like rain. There was a pungent smell of dirt, of grass, of my own sweat.

"That was something."

"I don't know what happened."

"You looked *possessed*, Kempton."

"I was scared shitless."

"I know."

It had showed, but I didn't mind—at least not if *he* knew.

He waited for me while I showered, then we walked across the fields to Jefferson, a light rain beginning to fall, a chill coming from the hills. Budlong stood in the doorway of his apartment. He was still in his coach's uniform but had loosened his belt and stood in his stockinged feet, his face strained and blotched. It would not have been surprising to any of us if that pleasant, sleepy exterior hid a different kind of man. We had heard rumors of drinking, of an unhappy marriage, and now, as if to confirm these suspicions, he looked belligerent and muddled. Andrews and I hurried on.

"I want to talk to you. No, not you, Kempton. Andrews, come in here."

I waited outside. The bells began to ring. Down came the mighty peals; through the thick, reverberating sound I heard a high-pitched cry from Budlong's apartment—a howl of pain, as though Budlong had struck Andrews with his belt or meaty fist. What could my friend have done? Andrews came charging out of the apartment door, his mouth open and all expression gone from his eyes. He was paler than pale; he did not see me. He lurched past and ran headlong back across the fields.

"Andrews? For God's sake, what is it?"

He disappeared behind the bleachers, then came into view again, jumping the stream. I saw him in the woods, climbing.

"Come on in here, will you, Kempton?" It was not Budlong's usual voice. His face had softened; he looked tired and old.

Lord Lochaber, Colonel Lord Lochaber of the British Fourth Armoured Corps, had been wounded in battle on the Rhine. Lady Lochaber had called from California; she was coming to New York; she and Andrews would go to London; special arrangements were being made. A shell had hit Lord Lochaber's tank, set it on fire; he had crawled out, half on fire himself. Fought in the entire war. One of their great heroes. Didn't know, did you, Kempton?

"Yes, sir, I did. Andrews worships him."

"Wouldn't tell him herself. Made me do it. Made a botch of it too. Poor fucking little limey."

I was out the door, running after him. Already the grass was slippery from the drizzle. I crossed the stream and started up through the woods. It was a steep path that climbed for two or three miles and came out onto high meadows. Beyond the meadows were more woods filled with ponds and toppled stone walls, and then the land pitched down into the next valley. I hoped he had not gone all the way up into the meadows, but I was prepared to follow until I found him. I could feel his wound in every drop of rain that came down, in every heavy step along the path.

"Andrews? Where are you? It's Peter."

At last I saw him. He was holding onto an old mountain ash by the side of the path. I put my hand on his shoulder, but he shrugged it off and stood with his cheek against the bark of the tree. "Andrews, are you all right?"

His breath came in gasps. He was wet; his hair and face and jacket were wet. He turned with a wail, blubbering and crying and reaching for me. "What will I do, what will I do? He's all I've got, he's my hooom. Oh, he'll dieee."

And as his voice faded away he clutched at my clothes. The rain came down more heavily, and we stood weaving on the narrow path until we heard voices. "Halloo? Are you there? Kempton, are you there?" From a far distance came the flickering of flashlights through the woods, and I shouted firmly, "Go away! Go away!"

In darkness we started down the path, slipping on leaves, branches stinging our faces. We came to the stream, crossed over, and confronted the empty bleachers. It wasn't until then that I realized my father had not come to see the game. Recalling my earlier triumph, turning to my friend wandering about dazed beside me, I had a thought that would shame me for a long time to come: Now you will know what it is like. Having uttered these words to myself, I tried to fling them away. I did not understand the varied ways of grief; I wanted only to still his sorrow, not knowing it would make mine flare up too.

"They're arranging a special plane for you."

"I suppose they are. My mother's good at those things. Look—what have we here?"

A tiny white object flitted along beside us. It had left the woods and was going along with us across the field. Andrews moved quickly, capturing it with a flick of his wrist and cupping it in his hands.

"Let's see what we have." He peered into the ribbed chamber of his fist. "Just a small egger. They hatch early; they come out at night to feed on the sweet stuff of the woods. Nothing remarkable."

We came to the grassy incline that led to our dormitory. I saw him raise his fist and clench it, but not in that intense way he had when he was fusing an idea into his very being. He was pulverizing the moth, crumbling it with his fingers so it would flutter no more. He dropped his hand to his trouser leg and let what was left of it—a few grains of dust—float down onto the grass. As I saw him do this, as I thought ahead to the time when he would no longer be there, I began to weep. I reached out for him, but we had already come to the path. The lights were on. Budlong was waiting by the door.

"My father will live," Andrews' letter read, "but he is most dreadfully burned. I can scarcely describe his condition without bursting into tears. You are the first person I have told."

26

THE WAR ENDED, but for me time stood still. My father did not come home from Washington. My mother stayed in her apartment, preoccupied and uncommunicative. The house on Long Island remained boarded up. It was rumored that my sister Susan, long a stranger to me, had fallen in love with a young man who worked in the War Department. And, most incomprehensible of all, my brother Randolph did not return from the Pacific, volunteering instead to join MacArthur's peacetime staff in Tokyo. No one knew how long he would stay. He wrote me often, and his letters frightened me.

When we started corresponding in the winter of 1943, he made the war in the Pacific sound like a movie musical. The airplanes had amusing mottoes scrawled across their snouts, and June Allyson was waiting cheerfully for Van Johnson during every furlough. But as the American forces moved across the vast ocean, and as Randolph and his fellow pilots flew more bombing missions, the tone of his letters grew more sober. Suddenly he was immensely responsive to my own moods: "I know what it is like for you, dear brother, in the Grover hills. There were times when I thought I would die there, although I never knew exactly what I would die of. Could it have been loneliness? Could it have been that bad? I would hear trains wailing down the valley and I wanted one of them to carry me off, anywhere but home. Have you ever felt that? I wanted to be carried away to the ends of the world. And now I am here, wishing I were lying in bed listening to your trains again. At least you have that. I miss you. Pray for me, old bean."

My brother and I held each other close in these letters, sharing our various lonelinesses. But gradually I became aware that there was something else he wished to share. He wanted an accomplice in his hatred for our father.

He told me that our father was cold. He hated the way he sucked up to Stim; he hoped I never sucked up that way to any of the Grover masters. He hated the way he spent money on things that showed, but nothing on those that didn't. Fräulein and Tony, for example, were paid coolie wages, and when the war came they were practically thrown out on the street. He hoped that we wouldn't turn out that way; he hoped we'd be generous—to underscore the point, he would send me a little pocket money. When my father asked if I had heard from Randolph (my brother never wrote to him), I replied almost gleefully: Yes, I heard from him all the time. And so, in a small way I became my brother's accomplice; but I was never comfortable in the role. I felt—as I was to feel in other things in life—caught in the middle, unsure of my ground, sharing the feelings of others but not as passionately as they.

When the war ended and Randolph witnessed the devastation he and his comrades had inflicted on the Japanese, his letters became a kind of catalogue of horrors. Of a young boy on a Hiroshima street he wrote, "His head was like a raspberry ice that had begun to run, then frozen, so the runny features were fixed in place forever." He could not seem to contain his rage—at himself for being party to this destruction; at my father and Stim and their kind, greedy bankers hungry for money and power. Alone, without Andrews, I walked the hills and fields of the Orion valley, trying to figure out how to respond. How was I to carry on a dialogue with a preacher so full of brimstone and fire? My concerns at Grover could only appear trivial to him. But I sat down and wrote about them anyway. And I told him how much I missed him, how I wondered when the family would come together, when he would come home to us again. For a brief moment I seemed to understand that he needed my voice. He had gone to the end of the world after all, and could not bear what he had found.

PART
III

27

I WENT TO Harvard and lived in an aerie on the top floor of Straus Hall. From my bed I looked down on the Square, amazed at the flurry and bustle. Even at midnight there were throngs of students milling about, new crowds pouring excitedly from the dark confines of the University Theatre.

My roommate was a flaxen-haired boy from Beverly Hills. After his first exposure to rain and the cosmic indifference of the authorities, he fled to the more sunny and maternal embrace of southern California. I never saw him again.

In order to be near his father, Andrews was attending the University of Edinburgh. I missed him. Loneliness intensified the fervor with which I threw myself into my studies. Part of my academic ambition was a matter of conditioning, part the influence of the war veterans, older and tougher than the rest of us and in my case surrogates for my brother. These were men, not boys, and they had fought at Anzio and Okinawa. Many of them were married; their pretty wives, some of them already pushing baby carriages, charged the atmosphere of the town with an almost unbearable erotic energy. The veterans had already lost years of their lives; they were determined not to lose more, and they brought to the lecture halls and libraries and graceful paths of the Yard a determination the rest of us had not encountered before.

There were others like me. God knows where they scattered when I began my descent into debauchery; after my freshman year I hardly saw any of them again. We sat earnestly and listened, transfixed, as our professors took the strands of philosophy and religion and literature and politics and wove them together—Good and Evil, the cathedral and the white whale, summer icumen in and ships a-sailin' out—until their discourse was like a tightly woven rope, strong and secure. In the magisterial humanities courses that took us from Aristotle to Eliot and from Aquinas to Freud, ideas rolled over us like towering breakers. We were tiny grains of sand—passive, porous, waiting for the pounding assault.

From this passionate flux, from this masterly reordering and reclarification, would come a truth; and the truth would illuminate the meaning of our lives. Secretly this is what I believed; this is what I hungered for. And others too. We were secret sharers, pasty-faced, ties askew, heads fallen on chests, pencils dropping. The Widener Library lights flicked on and off; it was time to go, time to gather our books. Dazed, demented, we walked under the bare elms of the Yard to our rooms, where the quest continued—a quest ostensibly for knowledge but in actuality for revelation.

My first grades were a triumph, surprising me and delighting my father, who sent one of his short, typewritten letters. Arthur wrote too—he was "proud." But when I went to Arthur's for spring vacation, he remarked that I looked a little wan. My father said sallow, during a brief lunch we had together. Like ranchers raising a piece of livestock for market, they approved the way I was growing; but the growth must be monitored, the calf mustn't fall ill. And so they telephoned me from time to time, to see how I was and what I was doing. I was surprised and pleased by their attention. And then on a breathtaking spring afternoon—the windows thrown open, the first bulbs up, the forsythia in bloom against the walls of the Yard—my father called again.

He called to give me the news of Randolph's death. A truck had struck his jeep in a traffic accident on a Tokyo street, killing him instantly.

I no longer heard sounds coming from the Square, no longer felt the gentle caress of that spring afternoon. I was no longer aware of anything but the wretched dryness in my throat and the uneven thump of my heart and my father's flat, controlled voice going on about the accident. Only later would I recognize it as the voice of someone choking on sorrow.

The coffin arrived at dawn. Four soldiers carried it smartly from the military transport plane to the hearse, which had come down from Ellsworth Falls the night before.

And so we began the journey up familiar roads—my mother, my father, Susan and I—following the hearse through Danbury, through Darlington with its tall elms, through Hollenbeck, Grover and Mercersville. Red barns and rushing streams and the old covered bridge made me want to lean forward and touch my mother, to put my head in her lap, to feel the pulse of her foot on the accelerator.

We arrived at the cemetery at noon. The soft May air, the freshly mown grass, the odor of the wet brown earth piled beside the open grave registered only briefly on the senses. Our family and friends were there: Arthur and Flint stood together; Aggie knelt and spread an armful of lilies next to the grave. Stim was leaning on his cane, heavier and older than I remembered, Joseph beside him in a tight-fitting black suit, a black hat clutched to his chest. Joseph was *elderly*. And the frail woman in the dark dress and heavy rubber-soled shoes? "Fräulein!" I cried, and lunged toward her, a child again—only now I was taller than she. It was I who held her, bony, wraithlike, her stringy hair quite white, her face as blotchy as though she had just turned from her stove.

Near the place where Randolph would lie were two low marble gravestones.

In Memory of
CLARENCE RANDOLPH STARCLIFFE
1852–1915
The spirit of the man is the candle of the Lord

Sacred to the memory of
LILA CONSTABLE STARCLIFFE
1860–1942
Jesus, take me dying to eternal life

John Nicholson, our Grover headmaster, stood in flowing robes, a brilliant purple sash draped diagonally across his chest. My mother and father stood next to him, my mother haggard, her deep-set eyes cast down. My father held my mother's arm, his knuckles white as gristle against her black suit.

"I am the resurrection and the life, saith the Lord! He that believeth in me, though he were dead, yet shall he live. . . ."

Nicholson's voice rang out across the valley like a clarion call. Outside the high iron fence of the cemetery stood the hearse and a line of cars; beyond them, a small house with gimcrackery around its porch, the sun glancing off its roof. Children shouted in the distance.

The war was over now; it had scattered us, then brought us together again, all but one.

"I will lift up mine eyes unto the hills; from whence cometh my help?"

My mother stood perfectly still, staring straight ahead, as though she too were not among us.

I could not concentrate on Nicholson's words. I could not look at the faces of my family or into the gaping hole. In a fleeting, disjointed fantasy, I pictured my mother and Susan and Fräulein opening up the house at Apple Tree Farm, flinging the shutters wide, Fräulein carrying cushions out on the lawn and beating the dust from them, my mother on her hands and knees bringing the cutting garden back to life.

At last Nicholson was done. One of the undertakers raised his hands and snapped his fingers. From my mother came a harsh, rusty sound, almost a croak. The other undertakers lifted the coffin and began to lower it into the hole. Could that really be my brother's body inside? Was it tanned and muscular as I remembered it? Was he dressed in his uniform? Nicholson picked up a morsel of earth and flung it down on the pine box. "Dust unto dust . . ." I felt my legs shake. Susan began to sob. Stim was beside me, his arm on mine, holding me as once he had held my father—long ago, before the war had begun.

Afterward in Flint's farmhouse, Stim limped through the small rooms and reached out to everyone—Flint, Aggie, Ned Willoughby, Grover masters, old friends. For each of them he had a few words, a moment of concentrated attention. It was only when he came up to Arthur that he seemed at a loss. My uncle turned quickly and walked away.

"Now it's just you and me, chum," said Susan on our last afternoon. We were sitting on the lawn in back of Flint's house, the shadows of the elm trees moving slowly toward us, the signs of spring on all sides. The others had left the morning after the funeral; only my sister had stayed the few extra days with me, and tomorrow we would leave too—she for Washington, and I for Harvard to finish the last weeks of the term.

I was immensely grateful for her presence and for the eager way she accompanied me wherever I wished to go. We picnicked in the meadow by the Kempton quarry; we walked along the banks of the Belledame to the old Starcliffe Works, a brick skeleton with gaping windows and crumbling walls. And that morning we made a pilgrimage to the Grover School, where my sense of cumulative loss, of Andrews as well as of Randolph, evoked a wave of sorrow that made her reach out and put her arm on my shoulder.

From the house came the sounds of a kettle singing. Flint had returned from his afternoon round of golf and was preparing a special herbal brew for his digestion. Before long he would bring it out onto the back porch and drink it while studying racing forms and stock market reports. Each morning he placed bets with his bookie and his broker.

Susan wanted me to come to visit her in Washington. Our father was away much of the time, so there would be room for me at their apartment. "I know some ravishing girls," she said, "and there's someone I particularly want you to meet."

My sister again wore her lovely brown hair in a soft, loose style. I could see her beauty in the shy, admiring glances of the Grover boys earlier that day. I could see it as she sat looking at me mischievously on Flint's lawn.

"What's her name?" I asked, a little warily.

"It's a he. And I'm thinking of marrying him."

Only the moment before she had been talking of the two of us, alone, against the world. I tried to hide my disappointment.

Susan had met him in the War Department several years before. Now he was returning to New York to join his family's investment counseling firm. Toby Fletcher-Harris was his name—preposterous name, I thought, and yet an oddly familiar one. My sister told me the Fletcher-Harrises had a huge estate about six miles from Apple Tree Farm. It came back to me—we had called them "the indoor-tennis-court people." They had squash courts too, and bred horses that fetched handsome prices at Saratoga. "Toby's got just oodles of money," said Susan. Her burst of laughter suggested she wasn't quite ready to permit me, and perhaps herself, to take the prospect of this liaison entirely seriously.

"Father will be pleased."

"We'll live in one of the cottages on the place."

Perhaps it was serious after all. Was Susan really to become one of the neutrons? What in the world would my mother think?

"As a matter of fact, the puppies are already there."

The puppies—why did those words fill me with such joy? Was I still as childish as *that*?

"What happened to François? Was he killed too?"

"Noooo . . ." Suddenly her mood darkened. She was no longer the confiding sister or coquettish fiancée.

"I didn't hear from him for a long, long time . . . not during the war, not even afterward. I was sure he was dead. And he very nearly was. He's home now at the château. We keep in touch."

"Are you still in love with him?"

"Oh, Peter, what a question!"

The shadows reached us. There was a chill in the air, and Susan was getting to her feet, smiling again. Although I was more suspicious of her smile now, I could scarcely quarrel with what she said. "I have a new life ahead of me. So do you!"

My uncle came out onto the porch with his steaming glass. He blinked at us through his bifocals, a little puzzled but obviously pleased that we were there. Susan went up to him and kissed him on the cheek and asked about his afternoon round.

In the morning we placed flowers on Randolph's grave and went our separate ways.

When I returned to school I found a letter from Stim—and a splendid invitation. He had chartered a sixty-foot ketch for the summer. Would I go on the shakedown cruise? He was starting from New London in mid-June, and if I liked, I could sail with him as far as Marblehead.

We had a glorious time, four days and four nights. Block Island, Woods Hole, Nantucket and the long run around the Cape in a heavy sea, beating into the wind, coming about and coming about, Stim buckled into a specially slung seat behind the helm, bellowing orders to the captain and the mate and me. In the evenings we rowed ashore and ate huge quantities of lobster and steak, Stim downing whisky and beer, encouraging me to join him until timidly, then with interest, then with pleasure, I did.

When we came up to our mooring in Marblehead Harbor on our last night, we were windburned, we had salt in our hair, fresh air in our lungs, a wonderful languid fatigue in our limbs. At dinner in the Pequot Hotel he proposed I come to work for him later that summer. He planned to be back in the city in two weeks. He pulled out his engagement pad and noted the day and told me to be there. The work wouldn't be exciting, but I could get a feel for the place. Boomer would organize things. He'd call her first thing in the morning. By the time we said goodbye we were like two old salts planning another voyage. The train came in, and he hugged me. Sliding away into the night, I waved from my open window and heard him shouting, cane lifted high, "Bon voyage! Bon voyage!"

When I arrived at 20 Pine Street, Boomer came down, consternation on her face.

"What are *you* doing here, Peter?"

I explained.

"Come to work? But he didn't say a word. And now he's gone off again. Oh, dear."

Which of us has not arrived at a place of new employment full of excitement, determined to demonstrate to one's employer that he has made a brilliant choice, only to discover the bitter truth about one's real role in the scheme of things? I concealed my disappointment and went about my duties as runner and mail opener and sometime guardian of the teletype machines. Stim would soon return and set matters straight. I would be stationed at his side to learn the business, as I had earlier that summer learned to come about.

I was baffled by the emotions my presence seemed to evoke. In the partners' room, the dark-suited elder men were mildly deferential, but I was as shadowy a figure to them as a doorman or a waiter. They remembered my name; they made polite small talk in the elevators; they thanked me a bit more effusively when I delivered coffee or mail than they would have had I not been, at least prospectively, one of them.

In the lower regions of the place, in the mimeograph room and the Cage, the men did not greet me when I arrived in the morning; they did not speak to me when we passed in the streets. When I mentioned these slights to Boomer, she replied, "You must understand, dear; we have had to let a few people go. The men are a little apprehensive." I was briefly reassured, but then someone let drop, after I had returned from Lehman Brothers without a receipt for a bearer bond, that my predecessor, an old runner named Bailey, would never have been guilty of such an error. I hadn't realized I had a predecessor, nor that I had replaced him; and I saw at once that I was a usurper, a privileged friend of the boss and would not be forgiven, no matter how well I performed. What saddened me most was that while I would remain an outsider among the clerks on the second floor, there was no compensatory companionship in the world of which I was, presumably, a part—the partners' room on the fifth floor where Stim and his peers made their home.

Arthur was shocked that I had gone to work for Stim. And this, in turn, shocked me.

For years I had known of the animosity between my father and Arthur, and between Arthur and Stim. But I did not have a clue as to what it was about. My mother ascribed it to a particularly virulent form of professional jealousy. She sometimes said that my father seemed *determined* to despise Arthur, as though he had never quite recovered from the humiliation of their first meeting. And Arthur's hatred of Stim seemed designed to get even with Henry. Anyway, it was one of those foolish things men were always getting upset about. But now, for the first time, it upset me too. I was grateful to Stim for offering me companionship that summer. I could hardly wait for his return. And so when Arthur asked me what I was doing at the Stimson firm, I lied to him. I did not tell him how mundane my tasks were, and how unfriendly my reception. When he brought up the subject of a training program—he was proud of the one at Grenfell, Starcliffe and Company—I made up a shocking fib about training at Stim's. The greater my enthusiasm, the darker his face grew.

Stim returned in mid-July. It was soon clear I was not high on his list of priorities. When finally I was ushered into his office, he spun in his chair and said, "Boomer taking good care of you? Finding your way about all right? Good boy." And that was that.

All the same, his return made a marked difference in the atmosphere of the place. His commands set off a jittery reaction that spread from the partners' room on five to underwriting on four to sales and syndication on three and finally to bookkeeping and clerical services on two. He summoned his associates in an imperious voice; he shouted and teased and barked and cajoled. All about him was a flurry of apprehension as flunkies ran to find out why the A account was short two thousand shares Anaconda; where the blazes was the RCA comparison; who said we weren't going to be in the National Cash deal? Schiff? Get him on the phone! The market's off six? Where's Steel? Where's Motors? What the devil's going on here?

Now the activities of the firm had a spastic quality, deadly calm giving way to shouting matches, frantic meetings, emergency shipments of documents to printers. There were more layoffs, and toward the end of the summer an awful hammering noise came from the third and fourth floors. Walls were being moved, departments consolidated so that space could be sublet after Labor Day. Stimson and Company was pulling in its horns. Soon it would be fighting for its life. Did Stim know? If so, I saw no sign of it, not a trace of worry or fatigue.

On Sunday mornings I went to my aunt's apartment and lay on the floor reading the newspapers and listening to Horowitz and Licia Albanese. I told Aggie that Arthur, discovering that I liked music, had asked me to accompany him to the opera at Christmas. I was taken aback; I didn't know he liked that kind of thing. "Why, sweetie," my aunt cried, "those are the ones who do—lawyers and bankers who've taken all the magic out of their own lives."

In early August my father came up from Washington to take my mother and me to *Annie Get Your Gun*. The war had been over for two years and yet he had not returned to his old job. He was involved in all sorts of international conferences, always traveling, always on the run. Now we were to have a splurge—dinner at Sardi's and the theater. It was, he admitted wryly to us, out of character. His joviality was a little forced. And my mother was strangely shy. She kept picking at the paint under her fingernails; there were little streaks of it in her hair too. Something was missing between my mother and father. The old tension was gone; but instead of peace, there was only emptiness.

When I went to say goodbye to Stim, he was as affable as ever. "Had a good time, my boy? Will you come back to us next year? Grand job you've done. Boomer's proud of the way you've taken hold."

I wandered down to Battery Park and ate my last lunch on a bench overlooking the harbor. All summer I had come here by myself, eating my sandwiches slowly, determined not to let the hostility of the men on the second floor get me down, determined to make it through the summer, even though the days were long and dreary. For the last time I watched the gulls wheel high above the ferries. Ocean liners were moving slowly near the Jersey shore. Here was one coming closer, moving across the harbor. Its horn bellowed; the ship shimmered in the summer haze.

I thought: Randy will never come home again.

28

WHEN I RETURNED to Harvard, I was no longer conscious of the veterans; I was no longer interested in my work. I did not see what lay ahead, and I didn't care.

I met Morley Moorcock on a warm October afternoon in the courtyard of Eliot House. He was giving a party. The gathering had started in his suite and overflowed onto the paths and lawns. The harsh, intoxicating sounds of "*La Vie en Rose*" came wafting from his living room, and Morley himself sat on one of his windowsills beckoning all passers-by to come have a brew. He dipped a silver ladle into the darkness of the room behind him and, like a conjuror transmuting the elements, brought it forth into the sunlight filled with a mixture of brandy and vodka and grapefruit juice. This he poured lovingly into little ribbed punch glasses arranged next to him on a stool.

He was a bright lobster of a boy with a rumpled thatch of curly red hair. He wore a heavy tweed suit with a vest, the buttons undone, his shirt billowing free. Before I knew it, he had filled a glass for me and another and was holding me by the arm and telling me how to prepare various exotic cocktails and all about the parties he had attended the night before, and in a great blurry rush I was hearing about his family —about cousins and maiden aunts and his "maw" and "paw." I stepped back to catch my breath. A window was opening on the floor above; figures leaned out, giggling. Morley tilted his head, and I thought that by some new act of prestidigitation he was about to ladle his lethal brew upstairs, but instead I saw the flash of a tilted glass bowl and a purple blur pouring down the brick wall like a spotlight. The punch struck him in the face and splashed over his suit.

"Yeah, Morley!"

He toppled into the bushes and hit the moist spring earth. We lifted him high and carried him to his room and laid him on the floor. A small glass was filled and brought to his lips.

"Here, Morley boy, here. This will make you feel much, much better."

Eyes closed, lips nibbling like a horse's at sugar, he sniffed and licked and took a small sip.

"Wha' is this stuff? . . . I'm gonnabesick. . . . I'm gonnapuke."

Through the open door of the john we saw him kneel before the toilet bowl, saw his head jerk forward.

"Oh, how awful," said one of the pretty girls.

"Where's Storey's party?"

"Lowell, B-31."

"Onward!"

Morley slumped backward and lay in a heap on the bathroom floor.

I examined the aftermath of the storm that had swept through the room. Dirty glasses and crushed napkins and twisted cigarette butts lay spread about. Holding my breath, I dragged the body out of the bathroom, across the living room into the small bedroom and up onto the bed. The odor of socks and unlaundered sheets had the tartness of a brewery. The form on the bed stirred; an eye opened, took me in, closed; the head turned toward the wall; snores began.

The next morning he knocked on my door; he stood there, insisting—was it penance?—that I accompany him to his parents' house for Sunday lunch. His convertible was outside. We went speeding up the North Shore; forty-five minutes later, in the town of Ipswich, we pulled into the drive.

Mrs. Moorcock came out onto the porch of the Victorian house that rose before us like an elaborate and implausible shrine. The shingled facade had been painted mauve, the woodwork was black; the patterned combination of the two gave off an odd glow not unlike stained-glass windows, at once luminous and opaque. Porches and corbels and rounded turrets soared toward the pitched mansard roof. I had never seen a house like this before; yet I felt I knew it.

Broad-shouldered and formidably bosomed, Mrs. Moorcock stood at the head of the steps. She was attired in a cardigan sweater and a skirt and sneakers. Her jaw and shoulders and hips proclaimed certainty, security, force.

"Maw, this is Kempton."

"Kempton who?" The voice came from her diaphragm, as though she had been taught as a young girl to "project" and had learned her lesson well.

"Peter Kempton," I said, sticking out my hand.

"Delighted, Mr. Kempton. Where are you from?"

"Long Island."

"Good gawd."

The light inside the hall came flowing in through shutters in the adjoining rooms. There was something almost aquatic about our reflections in the long mirrors as Morley and I followed along in Mrs. Moorcock's wake.

"Pudding, they're here," she proclaimed as we entered the library.

The man who rose to greet us was tall and thin and decked out in an elegant gray herringbone suit. He had a slightly dandified, melancholy air. How could he possibly be a match for Morley's mother? But when he greeted me in his quiet voice, when my eye darted over his head to a portrait on the wall of a similar but older man, long-faced, lean, with the same serious eyes, I saw that I was wrong. Mrs. Moorcock might be in command, but Morley's father *belonged.* This was *his* house; his father's before him. The books rising on all sides—Gibbon, Voltaire, Montaigne, Trollope, Melville, James—were his; and the forest of bottles and glasses before him like a chemist's worktable were emphatically his too.

"Dry martini, Mr. Kempton?"

He handed me a long-stemmed glass in which a lemon twist floated on a calm, oily surface.

"Watch Paw's marts," said Morley. "They pack a wallop."

Before lunch, martini in hand, Stanley Moorcock gave me a tour of the house. We started under a portrait of Morley's great-grandfather, a saturnine character in a frock coat, a lawyer—all Moorcocks were lawyers and judges. That was what Morley would be. We made our way into other rooms hung with ancestors and up the broad staircase, where against grass-cloth walls were arrayed a number of etchings and watercolors of Florence and Venice, precise, charming works produced by a distant cousin, one of the rare émigrés from the Bar.

On the mantelpiece of the master bedroom stood dozens of china and silver rabbits. I began to ask Mr. Moorcock about them, but he turned away and picked up a photograph of Morley and his younger sister, Alexandra, whom I had not yet met, an appealing tow-haired girl of thirteen, with a mouthful of braces. In the photograph she and Morley stood on an old wooden dock, both of them looking eagerly into the camera. The picture had been taken at Angel's, the family island in Buzzard's Bay. The Moorcocks went there every summer, and this next summer, Mr. Moorcock said, I must join them. I was immensely pleased.

We moved on through other rooms filled with canopied beds and unpainted wicker chairs and brassbound chests, none of these things handsome. But still I felt at one with them. And when we returned to the staircase and stood looking down into the lovely, moving sepia light of the hallway, I understood Stanley Moorcock's pride in this place. It was his sanctuary. With a surge of emotion I knew what this house reminded me of. It was a place I had never seen—my Grandfather Starcliffe's house on the banks of the Belledame.

I do not know when I first realized I had had too much to drink. Was it when I finished Mr. Moorcock's awesome martini and lurched down the hallway to the dining room, even more aware than before of the vibrations in the lovely light? Was it when I saw him begin to pour the second bottle of decanted claret, and the dining room with its pewter chandelier and brass sconces began to tilt?

As soon as we were seated at the round table they began to ask about my background. They seemed not at all taken with the Kempton side of the family, even though my father had Boston roots. It was the Starcliffes who interested them. Stanley Moorcock had heard of the famous patent fight at the turn of the century; he had heard of Arthur Starcliffe; his law firm had even done business with Grenfell, Starcliffe and Company. But they did not stop there. "Now tell us, Peter," said Harriet Moorcock, "what is your family really like?" And I was finally ready to tell. The alcohol loosened more than my tongue; it loosened all kinds of partly formed thoughts, which came as revelations. My mother and father did not get along; my mother and father quarreled incessantly, and he had once even struck her. The Moorcocks exchanged glances. My brother Randolph had despised my father. More glances. My mother had despised the strange crew that had come to Stim's. Led on by powerful new forces of recall and splendid new powers of articulation, I described —I cringe to think of it—how one moonlit evening I had followed the puppies into the woods and discovered a beautiful young countess swimming nude with her lover.

"My," said Harriet Moorcock, "it sounds just like John O'Hara!"

Morley laughed uproariously. "Maw, how would you know?"

"I read the reviews, Morley."

In the pause that followed, I said inanely, "This is a splendid claret, sir."

"Margaux nineteen thirty-eight," said Stanley Moorcock. "Last decent year before the Germans."

"Don't they live together?" asked Morley.

"Who?"

"Your maw and paw."

"Not for years."

"Poor old pudding," said Harriet Moorcock.

"Who?" I asked.

"Why *you*, of course."

In the car I tried to close my eyes. I had never admitted these things to anyone before, not even to myself. Now I had brought it all out, soiled laundry, and aired it before perfect strangers. When we were back in Cambridge, Morley said, "Maw and Paw were moved."

I was not at all reassured.

In the year after Randolph's death, Morley and I became friends. He was neither brave nor athletic nor scholarly, merely, I thought, himself—gregarious, loquacious, sentimental, boozy, disheveled. He farted and burped and got drunk and threw up. He smoked heavily, leaving a trail of ashes over his lapels and crotch. He slept late and missed classes. He ate prodigious quantities of take-out food and brewed evil punches and lethal martinis and fell asleep snoring on the floor of his living room. He resolved periodically to do better, to turn over a new leaf, to reform. These may seem odd qualities to be drawn to, but I was tired of heroes, and Morley suited me just fine.

In the late afternoons he would lie on my sofa and talk on the phone to his maw, the two of them a pair of cronies regaling each other with the events, large and small, of whatever day was winding to a close. He presented a litany of mea culpas and was scolded and forgiven. The conversations themselves were a form of forgiveness—indeed, almost a benediction.

If the qualities I have described are the ones that drew me to Morley, those that attracted me to his parents are no longer so easy to explain. I saw other boys come to Sunday lunch and squirm and blush and sometimes confess, as I had, under the spell of their curious curiosity. Stanley and Harriet Moorcock were like skilled surgeons, opening wounds, appraising them and—what was it, exactly, they did then? Did they excise and clean and sew? In my case, they did. Their solicitude had the power to soothe and heal. The fact that one could be made to reveal intimacies and then be invited back and implicitly forgiven provided a kind of reassurance that no other discourse would have yielded. I was not used to such bountiful interest.

29

IF ANDREWS HAD brought the observable natural world into my life, this was still a world in which he was more at home than I. But I was at home with him; and the two of us could face all the other worlds together—if from a certain distance.

With Morley the situation was quite different. Morley was interested in people, not in rocks or lichen or butterflies. The rest of Harvard beat a path to his door, guzzling his booze and listening to his records and accompanying us on our drunken jaunts. At first I was made uneasy by this conviviality. I felt that he, like Andrews, was the one who had forged the link. He belonged; he was sustained by the flow of people and parties, and I was sustained by him. Alcohol helped to ward off this feeling; in its warm glow I was sometimes reassured. I was not often drunk; less often was I sober.

"Kiss the Hare, Brer Kempton. Kiss the Hare. Kiss, kissss, *kisssssssss!*"

We had been led blindfolded through the wintry Cambridge streets in our flannel rabbit costumes. Now we stood wide-eyed with a handful of similarly garbed boys in a banquet hall swollen with toasting, staggering, tuxedoed men. Biscuits flew through the air. "Kissssss! Kisssssssss!" A black man in scarlet livery held a silver platter high; on it reclined a roast hare, apple thrust between its jaws. I leaned forward and planted my kiss on the animal's breast. "Say the words!" And I shouted, "*Dum vivimus vivamus!* While we live, let us live well!" "Never better, Brer Kempton. Raise the chalice!" The steward lifted the silver loving cup, counseling in a low, urgent voice, "Drink the whole bumpah, Brer Kempton. Drink up, suh." I raised the chalice and put it to my lips and drained it. Golden Gate, it was called, half beer and half champagne. I gagged but held on. "Hear, hear, Brer Kempton. Kiss the Hare, Brer Moorcock. Kissss, kissss!" Morley leaned forward and planted his kiss, a little saliva dribbling over the steward's scarlet tunic. The platter moved down the line of stunned boys. "Kiss the Hare, Brer Hallowell! Kissss, Brer Boyden! Drink up! *Say the words!*"

After the ceremony, there were astonishing faces in the receiving line—faces from the front pages of newspapers and the back covers of book jackets, the faces of eminent politicians and authors and judges of the highest courts of the land. Stanley Moorcock was there, and other Moorcocks I had not known of before. Just as Moorcocks belonged to the Bar, they also belonged to the Hare.

Snow coming down on a February afternoon. I am nervous about meeting my father for dinner at the Ritz. He has sent me one of his formal notes, *summoning* me, and I have come to Hare Hall to fortify myself. Morley and a few of the other newly elected Brers are playing billiards in the next room, and Amos, the steward, mixes drinks in a silver shaker. "Mo' cocktail, Brer Kempton?" I hold my glass out and gaze over Massachusetts Avenue to the low brick buildings that frame the Yard and watch the snow come down and cover the slate roofs and the sidewalks where freshmen are hurrying along.

I turn for a moment and study the room with its ornate painted furniture, its paneled walls hung with buffalo heads and oversized carved penises and turn-of-the-century paintings of rabbits romping with nude damsels in sylvan glades. Fluted brass columns support damask draperies over the bar. The place is like the camp of some primitive tribe, like a male seraglio, like a valentine. Violence and lust figure in the motley artifacts. But there is sweetness too—there is innocence in the gruff barking of orders, in the bawdy songs, the extravagant meals, and Amos's presence, shaker in hand.

Amos comes now and fills my glass again. I gulp the fiery gin. Is this to be a haven, this cozy, bizarre place with its coterie of brothers? Is the embrace of ritual and artifact and camaraderie enough? Already I know deep inside that they will not do. And yet I am reluctant to stop fondling the possibilities in my mind; I am reluctant to head out into the storm to face my father.

I get off the subway at Charles Street and walk to the hotel through the falling snow, hoping that the wind whipping off the river will clear my head. In the Public Gardens the paths are eerily still. My heart beats faster. I am cold and out of breath by the time I go through the revolving door of the hotel. I see him before he sees me. He is sitting at the far end of the bar staring at his drink, lost in thought.

I am eighteen years old on this snowy February afternoon. He is fifty-three, and I think of him as old. He looks older than I remember—hair grayer, face a little fuller and softer—but I know he will be formidable. I go toward him; still he does not see me. I realize he is a stranger. Part of me is glad, for I am afraid of him; another part of me, more hidden, is resentful. I have a grudge to settle, even though I am not sure whether it is mine or one that Randolph has bequeathed me. And if it is my brother's I am not sure what failure, specifically, my father is to be held accountable for.

There were many things I did not know about him as I walked through the darkened bar. I did not know, for instance, that he was still a youthful and vigorous man. I did not realize that to children parents are always old, and they are always pretty much the same, stuck with their samenesses, all their mannerisms and the ungraspable abstractions of their larger lives. I am sure I felt it was my duty to get out from under these familiarities. I was like a field mouse sticking its head out from a pile of brushwood and timidly weighing the advisability of a dash. I was conscious only of the weight of the pile and not of any of its redeeming virtues as shelter and disguise.

As he rose to greet me, I saw him deliberate whether to kiss me or to extend his hand. He extended his hand and said he was glad to see me; then he gave his sharp laugh and steered me to a table, his authority established in a flash.

We had a martini in the bar and another upstairs in the chandeliered blue-and-white dining room. At the far end of the room a turquoise-jacketed pianist played "Zip-a-Dee Doo-

Dah." Outside the snow came down over the Public Gardens and the sound of scraping shovels rose irregularly from the sidewalk. A white-haired man in a dark suit and a Phi Beta Kappa key on his watch chain came over from another table and greeted my father with obvious affection, asking when he planned to come back to Wall Street. "We miss you, Henry." After the other man had returned to his table, my father, obviously pleased, whispered that this was one of the senior partners of Morgan Stanley.

During dinner he began to talk about my bills. My grades had been falling and my expenses climbing, both at remarkable rates. I explained—I am afraid I was more than a little condescending—about the fall punching season and the requirement, now that I had made Hare, to pay my share of the bar chits, to attend my share of Hare dinners. That was really the point, after all, wasn't it, of belonging to a social club? To be social? Yes, he could see that. He had never belonged to such a club at Yale, and he was pleased now that I did. But still, he hoped I could be a bit more careful.

I was not used to this mildness from him. I had always steeled myself for his anger, and I was determined, as my brother would have been, to fight back, to hold my ground, to stand on my rights. It was not until dessert came that he leaned back in his chair and told me that he had decided to accept a job with the new World Bank. He was going to stay in Washington.

Among the many things I did not know about my father—oh, I knew it in a vague sort of way, but it meant nothing to me—was that he had worked for only one man, only one firm, for his entire business life, from the time he left Yale (only a little older than I was that night) until the outbreak of the Second World War. I had no conception of what a change like this would mean to him. I had no appreciation, either, of his wartime accomplishments. Unlike many of the businessmen who had gone to Washington, he had not settled for a leisurely life in a pleasant Southern town; he had gone to work with his usual determination. He had made a number of enemies, but more than enough friends and admirers too, to win this important new job.

I did not ask him what this job entailed; I did not congratulate him. I said idly, "Does that mean that Mother will go to Washington now?"

"That is what I have come here to tell you. Your mother and I have decided to be divorced."

"Divorced?"

"Yes. I am planning to be remarried."

He took a sip of water, looked at me uneasily and told me whom he planned to marry. I might not remember her—a lovely woman who had come to Stim's before the war, when I was little. Her name was Maude Lindenskjold. She remembered *me*. She loved him and he loved her, and he hoped I would do my best to understand and wish them whatever happiness I could.

"Countess Lindenskjold?"

"You do remember her."

Remember!

Laughter and gentle splashing in a pool; moonlight shining down. She came out of the water like a nymph. Was my father the shadowy figure behind her? So many years ago? And if he was *not*?

My distress must have showed, for he reached out to take my hand, and as I pulled it abruptly away, I spilled my wine. What would happen to my mother now? What would happen to Apple Tree Farm?

"I don't know what your mother will do."

"You've sold the house, haven't you?"

It was the only time he looked at all flustered. "You might say that."

"Father, what does that mean?"

For years I had longed for some explanation—if only they

had told me earlier, if only they had let me know when I went off to Grover that they would not be coming back together again! And in that shocked moment it was almost as though I were that small boy again, still wanting to do what I had never succeeded in doing—to break down the wall of his anger. But now there was only mildness and sorrow. I didn't care what kind of new wall he put up, I would smash it to pieces.

I was shouting. "What *happened*, Father? Aren't you going to tell me?" People at the other tables were staring; what would the man from Morgan Stanley think now?

"Ssshhh, Peter. Ssshhh."

I wouldn't let him put me off. "Oh, Father, what spoiled it? Tell me, Father, please." I wanted him to lash out at me, to tell me to be quiet, to put me in my place. But there was only sadness on his face, an immense melancholy I had never seen there before—whether for himself or for me, I did not know. I had the feeling that if we had not been sitting in the dining room of the Ritz Hotel, he might have gotten up and put his arms around me. But on I went, until at last I brought Randy into it. I told him of Randy's letters, of Randy's thoughts, of what Randy had thought of *him*. And then he put up both his hands to cover his face.

The next morning I lay on my bed listening to music, hoping my father would call and we could start again. I reached over to lift the needle from the record and made a scratch. In my vile mood I took the arm and jammed it down until the point of the needle snapped. Then I got up.

A few weeks later, a telegram came from Reno. My father and Maude had been married; he was moving into her Georgetown house and would shortly begin his new job. He sent me his address and telephone number.

30

AGGIE CALLED. She was wary of "clever Southern women who marry royalty," but she had had dinner with my father and his bride, and Maude really seemed very nice. "And God knows, she hasn't married royalty this time."

My sister told me the Countess was wonderful; everyone in Washington adored her. And she had offered her Georgetown house for Susan's wedding reception—after months of indecision, it seemed that my sister was finally engaged.

My mother was uncommunicative. She refused to discuss the divorce or the marriage; she refused even to mention my father's name. She painted and kept to herself—but that, as Aggie pointed out, was what she had been doing all along. Then one day in April she drove up to Orion County, bought herself a house, and went there to live.

The time for Susan's wedding drew near. My mother had promised that she would attend, but since the ceremony would take place in my father's town and the reception at his new bride's house, it was understood by all of us that it would be an extremely difficult moment for her. It was Aggie's idea that I visit her in her country place and then bring her down to New York. If I could get her that far, my aunt said she would take care of the rest.

I borrowed Morley's car and drove across the state, arriving in Orion in the late afternoon. Making my way through the familiar valley, I stopped first at Flint's to drop off my things. He gave me directions, and soon I found the dirt road that led to my mother's place. It ran along the west bank of the Belledame, the river winding through groves of pine and birch, flat wet stones shining brightly in the shallows. Up ahead there was a low wooden bridge. I rattled over its rough planking and came to the old mill house. It was set back from the river on a grassy bluff. My mother stood before an easel, paintbrush in hand, a bandanna in her hair. She saw the car and waved.

The scene was like a tableau, and I should have been suspicious of it. At a distance, I was only charmed. There was the house itself, its soft, fading brick covered with trumpet vine, its roof mossy, shutters bleached to cornflower blue. There was the river, willows along its bank, its pleasant murmur the only sound in this enchanted setting. And the view to the west: fields with slumbering cows; stone walls; low hills. One could even see a corner of the Dome.

My mother seemed happy to see me, and began showing me around. My heart sank when I saw that nothing had been attended to. Vines weighted down the old lilac bushes by the side of the house. There were piles of trash in the backyard; indoors, mouse droppings in the corners, and a powerful smell of mildew emanating from walls and floor, as though the place had once been soaked through and might never dry out again. My mother's painting things were strewn about; the turmoil of her New York apartment had simply been dipped in fixative and shipped up intact.

"I sleep over there," she said proudly, pointing to an unmade daybed in the corner of one of the downstairs rooms. "Flint says I'm an old hermit—one of those loonies in the hills."

I drove over from Flint's in the mornings and set about trying to tidy the place up, half expecting that she would give me a list of things to do. But she wasn't in the least interested. She disappeared down the river with one of her sketch pads, and a little later, she would be back again, standing before the easel on the lawn. She wasn't really paying attention to me when we sat having our sandwich lunches on the front steps. And when she began talking of her childhood, she abruptly stopped, as though her heart were no longer in the old stories. She sat silently, staring off at the Dome. Later there would be an unexpected flurry as she searched frantically for a brush or a tube of paint. I wondered then if my presence was partly responsible for these shifts of mood. She had come here to be alone, after all. She needed time to nurse her wounds and to work out a new pattern of life.

When I returned to Flint's he always asked how she seemed. Something in his tone reminded me of Arthur's attitude toward her; there was an old-maidish quality to their nagging concerns, and it made me spring to her defense. She needed time, I explained. And probably I was getting on her nerves. She needed to be by herself. Flint said testily, "That's the last thing in the world she needs."

The morning we were to leave for New York she was standing in her usual garb before the easel on the lawn. She would not look at me. She had decided not to go. She gave no explanations, just shook her head like a stubborn child and dabbed away unconvincingly at the canvas. It was only then that I realized how little work she had done. I came closer, to kiss her goodbye, and with a coy smile she twisted her face away. My lips brushed her hair. She had fooled us about coming to Susan's wedding. The look on her face made me wonder whether she had not also misled us in some other, graver way.

The brick of my father's and Maude's fine Federal house was the color of rouge. Aggie and I waited in the receiving line that started outside the front door and wound its way through rooms filled with graceful French furniture. There was a small Vuillard in the hallway, a Matisse odalisque in the living room.

"I'm glad your mother didn't come," Aggie whispered.

The Fletcher-Harris clan was there in force—as horsy as a gathering in a North Shore paddock. My new brother-in-law put one of his bearlike hands on my shoulder and shook it, welcoming me in this fashion into his manly, outdoorsy world.

And the countess? I had rejected my father's numerous invitations to visit after their marriage, not wishing to compromise the position I had taken, almost without realizing it, on my mother's side. Now that the time had come, I found I could hardly wait to see her.

She was just as lovely as before, with the same fine-spun hair and olive eyes. She gave me a radiant smile, and if she was aware of my attempted rejection, she took no notice of it and offered me only a deliciously perfumed cheek.

In the garden a small orchestra played waltzes under a striped marquee. The unexpected but familiar faces—a Cabinet officer, a congressman, a famous journalist—reminded me of the receiving lines at the Hare. Aggie and Arthur were talking on the edge of the gathering. Where was Stim? I was eager to see him, since he was always out of the country when I called Stimson and Company, and no matter how solemnly Boomer promised, he never returned my calls.

Maude and my father were mingling with the guests. She steered him over to my uncle and aunt. After they had chatted for a moment, she moved him on, guiding him adroitly through the crowd. She was in charge now. He was smiling; in a sense this was his celebration too.

My father had found the frame he was looking for, only it wasn't the frame of a painting, it was the threshold of a doorway. The door had swung open, giving him access to a new world, and he was striding into it, leaving us behind. Some such thought was in my mind during the drive back to New York. Looking at Aggie's plump, tired face, I wondered if it wasn't in hers too. Her brother wasn't coming back to

New York. And now my mother, her dearest friend, wouldn't be there either. Pragmatic and shrewd, Aggie could accept the Countess, but it was to my mother that her heart went out. Already she missed her; and she was more worried about her than she would say.

Neither of us in our wildest imaginings could have guessed that at that very moment my mother was back in the city, checking into a West Side hotel, where she would stay for the next two days making travel arrangements. Only then did she telephone Aggie to tell her that she was on her way to Paris. Would Aggie please drive her to Idlewild? She was terrified of flying; she needed someone to bolster her courage.

The two women had drinks in the airport cocktail lounge. My mother seemed to be looking for someone—almost, my aunt thought, as if she expected to be joined on her trip. Her fingers kept fastening and unfastening the clasp of her purse. "She was a bundle of nerves," Aggie told me. "I almost didn't let her go." My mother talked about her painting, about the need, if she were to do her work properly, not only to be alone, but to be far away. "But Sarah, why?" Something had happened to her. At first my aunt thought—God forbid—that she had had a revelation; but no, it was not that kind of thing at all. Had it happened just now, or some time ago? Agatha couldn't make out. A promise had been made, and then broken. But by whom? "Were you betrayed by Henry, Sarah? Why don't you stay, dearie, so we can talk about it? Why do you have to go off this way?" But my mother put her fist to her mouth. She had given up part of her secret and would give up no more. "She gave me the funniest look," said Aggie. I knew that look—the naughty child again.

A few weeks later, Agatha and I received postcards from Paris. My mother had enrolled in an art school. There were doves on the windowsill of her room on the rue du Bac. The Seine was lovely in the summer light, and she thought she would do good work now.

The cards were identical, but they came as a relief. Perhaps my mother had been right; perhaps she had needed to leave the world of her past and to make an entirely different kind of start.

I would not see her again for more than a year, and by then we would both be greatly changed.

31

I SPENT THE summer with Flint—an endless succession of quiet days with this quiet man who did crossword puzzles and played golf and worried about his digestion and wagers. Once a week he sat down and wrote to my mother. She never replied.

In mid-September I went to visit Susan in her new home on Toby's family's estate.

As I walked up the path, she came out of her rose-covered Norman cottage to greet me. The poodles bounded past her; they leapt into the air, and I let them push me over and lay helplessly on the grass while they licked my face and pressed their wet black noses against my side.

"They remember!" I cried. "Susan, they actually remember me!"

"So it would seem," she said happily. "Come on in. Toby's waiting. We're dying of thirst."

At dinner Toby provided a cheerful monologue about the prospects for the Yale football team and the stock market and a pair of week-old foals. Susan seemed perfectly content to let his hearty enthusiasm wash over her. She smiled at him affectionately; she summoned the maid with a little brass bell by her side; she poured the coffee from an antique silver pot. I couldn't tell whether she was truly in her element or thought the whole thing a delightful lark.

It was Toby who insisted upon showing me the wedding pictures, giving a running commentary as we leafed our way through the album. He and Susan looked like *Town & Country* models ready and eager for a succession of costume changes. When we came to a photograph of my father and Maude, arms linked, in the Georgetown garden, I was brought up short by how young and beautiful my stepmother was. I could not for the life of me see what she found so attractive in him.

"I can't imagine why Stim didn't come," said Susan. "He didn't answer the invitation; he didn't send a present. I'm still miffed—I've avoided Excelsior like the plague."

I hadn't heard from Stim either. But I knew there had to be a good reason why.

"Oh, Susan, let's ride over tomorrow. Let's find him."

We set out after breakfast. The poodles trotted along beside us; they had recovered their dignity, they were elegant and proud. The whole early autumn landscape seemed to have melted in a blaze of yellow leaves.

Susan was still complaining about Stim. When she finished with him, she turned to our mother. "Of course I knew *she* wouldn't show—what a coward!"

When I protested, she threw her hand out in disgust. "She's run away again. It's all she ever does."

"And I suppose Father's perfect?"

"What's that supposed to mean?"

"Shacking up with Maude all those years?"

"Oh, don't be such a prig. You sound just like Randolph."

She gave me a startled look, as though not quite believing what she had said. We rode on in silence.

A *For Sale* sign was staked out in the tall grass at the driveway to Apple Tree Farm. I was puzzled, for I thought my father had already sold the house. We walked our horses slowly up the overgrown avenue of copper beech. I had seen the house boarded up and the sudden burgeoning of thicket and vine during that last summer with my mother, but still it was a shock—the shutters of the house banging loosely, the greenish sludge at the bottom of the swimming pool, the way the whole orchard seemed to have toppled over, the trees torn open under the burden of unpruned branches. Susan looked absolutely stricken. "Oh, Peter," she said mournfully, "I don't know if I can bear this." We poked around in a desultory fashion and then made our way briskly through the pine woods to Stim's. But here too was abandonment. We looked in disbelief at the fallen grape arbor by the side of the tennis court. The Great Lawn with its chiseled maples was a lawn no more, only a shabby meadow. Was it so much smaller than I remembered because I had lost the eyes of my childhood or because the trees, unchecked now, were dwarfing the place?

We went around the back of the house and down to the stables. There were no signs of life—no horses in their stalls, no silver Bentley, no Slater. And when we rode back up to the front courtyard of the house we found a moving van parked there. I looked for Joseph. Instead, there were unfamiliar faces, workmen in overalls carrying large pieces of furniture across the cobblestones. I saw the chair with the drawer, saw in the arms of two men, their colors dazzling against the early autumn foliage, a pair of brilliant blue-and-white vases.

The mystery was solved almost before we knew it, leaving a darker—and to me, more troubling—mystery in its place. Toby was waiting for us at the stables when we got back; he was waving the morning paper. We both thought he was delirious about the score of some game. "Look at this. You won't believe it." The headline on the front page of the *Times* read:

New York Banking Firm
Declared Bankrupt
Stimson and Co. Closes Doors
Controversial Financier Vanishes

We rushed to the house to call our father, but he wasn't in the least helpful. Susan said she couldn't make him out; he sounded both pleased and angry.

No one else shed any light on the matter. Toby called his Wall Street pals. I called Aggie, and Aggie called Arthur: "Your uncle is being extremely close-mouthed. That usually means he knows more than he's letting on—but of course he always knows more."

It was rumored that millions had been lost; rumored that Grenfell, Starcliffe and Company was putting together a consortium to protect the small investors; rumored that Stim had been seen in Zurich, in Rio de Janeiro. But no one could get a word out of my uncle or anyone else on Wall Street.

Then the speculation died down. I was still deeply concerned. I cared for Stim; I missed him; I wondered where and how he was—and foolishly I called the firm and I called Excelsior, knowing it was futile, but still hoping I would hear a familiar voice—Boomer or Joseph—to set my mind at ease. But the phones had been disconnected, and it was in vain.

Each time a flash of lightning illuminated my life, someone had moved away—my mother, my father, Susan, and now Stim. It was with a sense of relief that I returned to Harvard that fall. Here would be golden clock towers and friendly paths and familiar routines, and, at the center of it all, my friend Morley.

He greeted me at the door of our new Eliot House suite with a sheepish look. He mumbled a few words, and then the bathroom door opened and out came a pretty girl.

"Peter, this is Kate Wingate."

I had seen her in classes and on the paths of the Yard. I had noticed the springy halo of blond hair, her shapely bosom, her lovely, long-legged walk.

The autumn was full of little awkwardnesses. Kate was always in our rooms, or about to be. No, Morley couldn't go to the Hare, he and Kate were studying. No, he couldn't go to the U.T. to see the Rita Hayworth, he and Kate were having dinner with her mother. And yet when the three of us were together, she and I were the ones who talked. She played the violin in those days, and so we talked of music—and of painting and books. Morley knew nothing of these things; his interest was only in family and friends.

"So you know our dear Kate," said Harriet Moorcock when I joined them for Sunday lunch. And Stanley Moorcock proceeded to explain the way the Wingates were related to the Hallowells, the Hallowells to the Lymans, the Lymans to the Moorcocks—an intricate piece of social engineering that made Morley and Kate distant cousins.

Sandy Moorcock was frequently at these lunches now. She was fifteen years old and counting the weeks until her braces would be removed. I felt she was there for me. It meant that Morley and Kate could go off by themselves after lunch and I would not be left alone.

So I took my meals at the Hare and ordered the young Brers about. They could be made to attend classes and take notes, to carry food and drink to the Hutch, the room on the roof of Hare Hall where the elder Brers went for their afternoon naps. They could be fined and cajoled and made to convince themselves that defeats were victory, hardships joy and petty despotism only an affectionate disguise for brotherly love.

I did not mind Morley's falling in love, for I knew it could not last. What would Kate Wingate do when she grew accustomed to his spectacularly lackadaisical ways? She would look up from her books, stare across our disheveled living room, and her green, slightly myopic eyes widening, she would see—of course, me. I was not alone in harboring such illusions. Nor was I alone in failing to ask why, if I loved Morley, she might not love him too. And yet, while she loved him for the same reasons as the rest of us, she began little by little to change him. He became—I can hardly bear the word —heroic. And so I lost them both, the beautiful girl and my friend. It did not happen all at once, but by the time spring came he had bought his new suit and started going to class and writing for the *Crimson*—and they were engaged.

Once again my father came to the Ritz, this time to read me the riot act. My bar bill at the Hare had run over three hundred dollars since Christmas. "I will not have it," he said, as we sat having dinner in the room overlooking the Public Gardens. I took in his finely tailored suit—this immaculate new European look of his, the cuff links, the custom-made shirt, the Italian shoes. Maude's influence. She had taste, you had to say that.

"But Father, what is the point of having so much money, if it worries you so?"

"I have less money than you imagine."

I thought if I played along, a little repentant, he would pay up. I was wrong. He informed me that he would continue to pay my tuition, but as for the rest of the bills, not a cent more.

"But I have no money, Father. None at all."

"Here," he said, "this will help." He handed me a small

embossed savings-bank passbook. Stim had made the first deposit—a thousand dollars—the day I was born. In subsequent years my father and Stim had added to it, and the interest had been compounding.

"It is yours. To draw on as you wish."

I looked for the balance. It stood at eight thousand dollars. It seemed a fortune, and yet, like the end of the world. My father was cutting the purse strings; he was teaching me my final lesson about the meaning of money. But when I looked at him, there was only distress in his face.

"I am truly sorry," he said, "that there is not more."

32

WITH MY NEWFOUND gains I paid off my Hare debts. I also bought myself a car—a Ford convertible, fire-engine red, with black leather seats. I would take off, putting Morley and Kate behind me, and head west past Newton and Dedham to the small towns along the northern rim of the state, the wind tearing at my face, the engine roaring, the little car tilting like a sailboat as I accelerated into the curves. Dusk came. I stopped at roadside taverns and drank at the bar, staring at myself in the tinseled mirrors, a serious, square-faced youth, already a little flushed and bleary from whisky. It was astonishing to be free in this manner, to be on the road, to be alone in these backwater towns. On I went, flying along. But later in the evenings my spirits flagged, and I had difficulty holding to the road. So I would bring my car to a halt and sit quietly on the edge of a village green and study the silhouettes of the handsome houses, the placement of windows and chimneys, the shape and character of pediments and gables and jetties. I did it solemnly, as my mother might have done it, out of a craving for something beautiful and secure. I was enraptured by shape and texture, by the mysterious correlatives of stress and support. Once or twice I even opened the car door and walked furtively across the quiet lawns and stood in the shadows of houses, trying to take sustenance from their durability.

The shutters in the Moorcock house had been thrown open and light poured in. An orchestra played in the front hall. Champagne flowed from a bar on the back porch. It had flowed at the Hare the night before, it had flowed all week long as we stood on chairs and toasted Morley and sang ribald songs and slew each other with our daring matrimonial innuendoes.

"Dance with me, Peter," said Sandy Moorcock, and off we went to the "Carousel Waltz." "Won't they make the happiest couple in the world? Isn't she the prettiest bride you've ever seen? You are coming to Angel's this summer, aren't you, Peter?"

"I'm going to Scotland, Sandy, to see my old friend."

"Scotland? Well, come to us when you're back. Promise?"

One of the other ushers cut in.

"Are you sure you have the right person, sir? Surely there's been a mistake."

They went galloping through the other dancers, Sandy smiling back at me. Her braces were gone. I'll keep my promise, I thought; I'll see you at Angel's. And I'll send you a postcard from Scotland. I was very drunk. I'd been plastered for a week.

It was after dark when I returned to Eliot House, took in the forlorn end-of-term look of our rooms, and slumped into a chair by the window. Arthur was expecting me the following afternoon in New York for a brief visit before I left for Scotland. I didn't want to go. I didn't know what to do or think about anything. I would graduate in a year. Then what? I'd have no money left—it was slipping through my fingers like sand. The prospects were dismal. It was too early to sleep. I didn't feel like seeing anyone. I thrashed around the place trying to shake my gloom. I do not know what hour it was when I made my way from the room to my car in the courtyard below. I do not know whether my new destination was then fixed in my mind or whether it came to me on the road. Did I drive in my usual hellbent fashion? Or was I more cautious and contemplative? Again I do not know, except that there came a moment when I was sure where I would go, sure that it was the only place. I could not be found there; I could be alone.

It was shortly before dawn that I broke into my mother's house and fell onto her bare cot. Animals scurried across the floor; branches slapped against the window frame.

In the morning the rain came. Water dripped from the ceiling, dampness came up from the cellar and chilled me to the bone. I found a blanket and wrapped it around me and lay shivering on the bed. I could sleep forever—no one would find me here.

On my second day I went to the local store and bought cheese, salami, crackers, a bottle of whisky. I came back and lay in the grass. The sun was coming out, drying things off. I listened to the pleasant sound of the river, and nibbled at my food and drank, and fell asleep thinking of Morley and Kate, lying on a beach in Bermuda.

The following night I drove to the Crossing, a bar by the railroad tracks in Hollenbeck. The place had had a notorious reputation in my Grover days. Liquor was served freely to minors, and single girls came there from the hosiery factory down the river. It was off-limits to the students, and I had never been there before. I did not at first recognize the face that stared back at me from the mirror behind the bar—the gaunt, unshaven face of a bum. My clothes were filthy. I sat there drinking the night away, the trains passing by, red lanterns revolving and throwing crimson patterns against the stained plywood walls of the bar. These were Randy's trains and mine. When they closed the bar, I staggered to my car. I jammed my foot down on the accelerator and lifted it off, hilariously imitating my mother's driving style.

Down her road I went, the car shimmying wildly in the sandy ruts, dust billowing up over the windshield and into my eyes. The bridge was just ahead. With a roar we went across, the car and I. There was the sharp sound of timber cracking as we went through the rail and began to fall. I felt a stab of bitter cold. Was it water? The force of a blow? I remembered nothing more.

It was Flint who found me, Flint who drove down once a week to keep an eye on the place for my mother. When I came to in the Ellsworth Falls Hospital, Flint's and Aggie's and Arthur's faces peered down at me, and Ned Willoughby's hand was on my brow. When she saw me open my eyes, when she heard Ned say, "He'll be all right now," Aggie leaned forward and embraced me and whispered, "Oh, thank the dear good Lord."

I felt that my head had been split asunder. But I had only a concussion, and bruises from head to foot.

When I was well enough to be released, Aggie came again and drove me to the city. I recuperated at her apartment, sitting quietly and listening to music. It was there that I began my preparations for Scotland. During those several weeks none of the people who saw me—Aggie, Arthur, my father, Susan—said a word about my behavior. I knew I had been drunk not for days, but for weeks—ever since the early spring. But the subject never came up. No one suggested I not have a cocktail; no one suggested I pull myself together. No one pointed out, as I was sure they would, what a botch I had been making of things.

I was grateful for their silence. It was not until I was on the plane that I realized that silence could hold so many things—so much reproach, and so much love.

33

WE SPENT OUR first day in Edinburgh, Andrews striking out through the broad streets as briskly as through the Grover countryside. The wind whipped into our faces as we stood on Castle Rock and looked down at the gray city and my friend explained in his pleasing voice, always glancing to make sure I was interested, about the various Davids and Roberts and Duncans who had played a role in the formation and defense of the place. He was as quick and intense as before but now had a softer, surer smile, and his quietness had in it new qualities of forbearance. I was happy to see him again, happy to listen to his stories, and even though I felt a little disoriented by my first tangible exposure to a past this dark and deep, there was reassurance in his voice and in the timelessness of all the Scottish intrigue and upheaval. When we returned that evening to his father's handsome Adam house in Charlotte Square, I lay on my bed while he pulled off my shoes.

"Oh, Andrews, what a splendid day!"

In Inverness his father waited for us at the head of a flight of stone stairs, the silver sprockets of his wheelchair gleaming in a sudden burst of light as the sun freed itself of lowering clouds. His calmness was like a pallor, his voice soft and a bit slurred. But the smile was Kenneth's, the flesh around his eyes crimping with a little spurt of tension and pleasure. "Come," he said, "it's chilly. We'll have some tea, or whisky, or gin, or whatever."

Kenneth stood behind the wheelchair and rolled him along through an immense vaultlike interior. "Chinese Gothic," he said in a stage whisper, and Lord Lochaber said, "I heard that. Your great-grandfather's doing, not mine. Too late now."

The small apartment in the rear of the castle was a friendly place with fireplaces blazing away.

"Is this better, Mr. Kempton?"

"Much."

"Like home, eh? My wife is in love with America. *Voilà*, America!"

Plump young women brought tea and scones; a little while later they came with whisky. The conversation was humorous and relaxed. Kenneth had bought newspapers and magazines in Edinburgh and read aloud from them to his father, who had difficulty seeing. They made caustic observations about politics; they considered the latest developments in the natural sciences; they agreed to send away for new books from Blackwell's. Indeed, they seemed wholly involved with the affairs of the world; and yet, as I looked about me at the small apartment and the arching corridors through which we moved on our way into the dining hall, I had the sense we were far removed from the rest of life.

At the dinner table Lord Lochaber spoke sympathetically to me about my brother's death and my mother's and father's parting of the ways. There was none of the Moorcocks' surgical scraping, only an unexpected tenderheartedness that left me much moved. Then abruptly he fell silent. He was brooding about something. His son brought him up sharp. "Don't be maudlin, Father."

His thoughts returned to us. "I'm not maudlin, Kenneth. I

only wanted Mr. Kempton to know that I understand some of life's disappointments." He turned to me. "Living here does strange things. This house is vast and old. The landscape is infinite. You will see it for yourself these next few days. I did not want you to feel disturbed or lonely. I mean only to make you feel at home."

"Thank you, sir, I do."

If there was self-pity in his ruminations, this was the only inkling I had of it. I thought it more likely he had made a shrewd assessment of my own unquiet condition. What he said was true—there was a quality here (I had felt it at Castle Rock) that altered one's sense of time and space; or perhaps these things were themselves changed.

When I brought up the subject of my Uncle Arthur, Lord Lochaber brightened. It was clear Arthur had made an impression. The men at the Scottish trusts did not suffer fools gladly; they had their guard up—especially against the Americans with their beguiling optimism. But Arthur had come prepared, and what Lord Lochaber remembered was the way he had kept them informed about their investments after his return home—not just for a month or two, but a steady stream of memoranda, for years. Yes, I said, my uncle was a meticulous man.

"Steadfast is the word I would use."

In the sitting room after dinner, he seemed more frail and tired. As Kenneth read to him he shifted his weight uncomfortably from one bony buttock to the other. He tried to steady his hands on the arms of his wheelchair. His eyes closed, and at length his head pitched forward. "I must wheel him off to bed now," said my friend.

In the morning we went to Culloden. Bundled in cashmere sweaters and a bright tartan scarf, Lord Lochaber—animated and refreshed—described the fateful rout of Bonnie Prince Charlie's Highland forces by the Duke of Cumberland two hundred years before. Open fields stretched away to the River Nairn. Farmers worked the meadows with wooden-handled scythes; the women in their bonnets were like peasants in a Millet drawing.

The next day Kenneth and I piled suitcases and fly rods and butterfly nets into the trunk of his two-seater MG and off we went down the driveway with a roar. At the gate we turned and waved to Lord Lochaber, who sat in his chair at the head of the steps. He raised his hand and let it fall.

We swept along across mountain ranges and broad green valleys where rivers meandered to the sea. Always Andrews was reaching out to touch me, to point out castles and herds of long-haired cattle and lochs green as serpents' skins. In the late afternoon we drove across a vast tundra that was like the swelling of a chorus, and then we dropped to the coast to a small village with a narrow main street, shops, a pub, a post office and our destination: a homely, high-roofed, stuccoed hotel, which, Andrews informed me, had once been a fishing and hunting lodge for Queen Victoria. It had only recently been opened to the public—"in about 1910."

From my room on the top floor, I saw a meadow filled with Shetland ponies. Gulls wheeled over a promontory. All these things were bathed in a remarkable hovering glow; I could not tell whether it came from the heather flung here and there or from a throbbing conjunction of light and water at the edge of the sea; in it, as Lord Lochaber had predicted, I saw infinity.

We spent the week hill-walking and fishing in an emerald loch under the brow of Dum-Spaulding. We glided for hours in flat-bottomed skiffs, our gillies crouched in the bows, paddling with wide, short-stemmed oars.

"If your gillie takes a fancy to you, he'll be your slave," said my friend. "He'll take you to the right spot, he'll tie your fly and practically cast the line for you. But if he doesn't find you sympathetic, oh, how long the days will be! These old fellows remember my father. What *we* do doesn't matter. He came here with his friends before the war, and of course they adored him."

On our last day we rode horses along the coast. Dunes towered over the sea. Marshy inlets blossomed with sand-pipers and terns, their wings spreading like the feathers of burst pillows. The air was warm, so we dismounted and swam. Andrews foraged at the base of the dunes for plants and small living things while I skirted the water's edge for shells. Everything here—birds and sea and sky and shells—was finely shaded. The lovely edges of our perception were sharp and the objects of our perception had not yet had their delicate markings rubbed away.

That evening, sitting in the paneled bar with its coal fire and display cases of snowy owls, Andrews told me what I had already suspected, that his father was dying. It had nothing directly to do with his war injuries, but they had weakened him, they had played a part. He had known of it for several months; he had not wished to cast a pall over my visit.

We went into the dining room and sat quietly together. I did not know when I had had such a happy and peaceful time as during this week. The infinity of which I had had a glimpse along this stretch of sea had nothing to do with past and future, of days lost and those to come, but only with the inexhaustible bounty of the here and now. My friend had shared his gifts with me again. I tried to tell him what his friendship meant; and that I knew what the loss of his father would mean, thinking, after all, I already knew of these things. As I began to praise him for staying near his father these last years and not going to Oxford, as he had dearly wished to do, he put his hand out and said, "I knew the day would come when I would miss him; but, you know, I didn't wish him to miss *me*."

On our drive back to Edinburgh, where I would catch the plane for London and for home, I thought of the wars there had been, of the battlefields and gravestones in this placid country where the firths and folds were so pleasing, the mountains and skies and fields so manifestly soothing they belied the possibility of injury or of death. I thought of all our losses and of what Andrews had said the night before. There was not only his loss to consider, but his father's. Without knowing it, I had become enfolded in my own sense of loss; I had not seen that my mother and father had lost Randolph too; my mother had lost Susan, my father, apparently, me; and they had lost each other and their home. As the sun came out and gilded the land in a way that could only break one's heart, I wondered why I had not seen these things before.

In London I changed my plans. I decided I would go to Paris to find my mother. Whatever the reason—however willful or foolish or brave she might be—she was of all of us the one who had lost the most and who was the most alone.

It took me a long time to make my way from the airport to my mother's hotel in the Seventh Arrondissement. I spoke no French and was startled by the bad-temperedness of the inhabitants. At last I found her street and then her hotel, in a charming block fragrant with fresh bread and coffee and cut flowers. It came as a shock to discover she no longer lived there.

The woman behind the desk hardly looked up. She unleashed a torrent of French, all of it angry, but then they all seemed to be angry. After it was clear I did not understand a word, she grumbled and wrote the name and address of another hotel, handed me the slip of paper, and escorted me to the door.

The second hotel was a run-down affair in a less beguiling street near the Sorbonne. There was another intimidating woman behind the desk in the tiny lobby. I was reminded of Boomer and her officious ways. Like Boomer, the guardians of these establishments wanted no part of young strays. They would shunt me from hotel to hotel, each smaller and more disreputable, until— but my thoughts were interrupted by the woman before me, the proprietress, it turned out, who gave a little cry of relief when she understood whom I had come to see.

She took a key from one of the cubbyholes and marched me up the narrow stairs. When we reached the top floor, she unlocked the door and without knocking swung it open and stepped aside.

My mother was sitting by an open window through which I saw pale-blue sky, hooded chimney pots, tiled roofs, geraniums, balconies, pigeons. It was the view she had described in her infrequent postcards, a view that came to mind when one thought of living in Paris. She was sitting perfectly still. I could not tell whether she had fallen asleep, but I had a presentiment—something in the hunch of her shoulders, the tilt of her head, suggested that she had been invalided. I moved forward and saw a low table in front of her chair, an egg, a tangerine, a slice of cheese—all untouched. And then I saw the crumbs, bread crumbs on the sill and the table and the carpet and the unmade bed. She had been feeding the birds. At that moment a pigeon came fluttering down and strutted about on the sill, prepared to come right into the room; seeing me, it beat its wings huffily and moved off. The litter of the room was like the house on the river, only the squalor had been compressed and intensified. The sour odors were those of a derelict old woman who lived alone with her cats, only there were no cats; my mother despised cats. These were the odors of her life, and scattered before me was its sickening debris, the familiar detritus of her craft, no canvases now, only old pieces of yellowing newspaper—the Paris *Tribune, Le Monde*—across which she had made a few desultory strokes with her crayons. The blur of my tears prevented me from seeing more.

I touched my mother's shoulder. Her head turned. Her hair had not been washed in some time. It looked like Fräulein's hair. She had lost weight, and the skin of her face fell away in colorless folds.

"Mother, it's Peter."

"Peter?"

"Mother, I've come to take you home."

After a silence that I thought would last forever, a silence in which I took in once again the awful details of her condition and her surroundings, she asked a question I had thought belonged only to me. It was my own secret question, tended like an exotic plant in a private garden, and I had never dreamed she ever asked it too, a single word, uttered so softly I could barely hear it, and yet it resounded against the peeling walls and floated out across the rooftops for all to hear.

"Home?"

Child that I was, I resolved that neither of us would ever ask it again.

At the Grenfell office on the Place Vendôme I found a Monsieur de Chauveron who spoke perfect English. He had been worrying about Madame Kempton; she had not come for her check in over a month. He thought she had gone to the country to paint; she often talked of doing this in the early days. He accompanied me to the hotel and spoke at length with Madame Brühl, the proprietress, whose spirits improved when she learned that her lodger would soon be gone. No, my mother hardly ever left her room; she no longer attended class; no, monsieur, she was never violent. A doctor was fetched, pills prescribed, a cable sent to Arthur. A woman brought new clothes and helped her to dress. Would she be all right on the plane? Yes, she was like a lamb. All the while the arrangements were being made, my mother sat by the window. She was like a figure in a painting, a still life. She had gone into the canvas and come to the place she wished to be.

When we landed at Idlewild there was a stain spreading over her skirt. I helped her put on her raincoat so no one would see.

Arthur stood at the foot of the stairs with a nurse and a shining limousine. I had never been so glad to see him in my life.

"Hello, Sarah," he said.

"Hello, Arthur. I'm terrified of planes. I do hope I won't have to fly."

"Of course not, Sarah dear. Not if you don't wish to."

Aggie had told me once that the only thing Arthur knew how to dispense was honor. But when he took my mother into his arms and held her, I saw he knew something of love —and with all my heart, I hoped salvation too.

34

MY MOTHER WAS taken to Liggett's, a sanitarium in Orion, a pleasant-looking place with handsome clapboard houses and old elm trees and well-tended lawns. She was given many examinations, many treatments, and her illness was described in different ways in a terminology that has become increasingly familiar with the years. She was placed in Ned Willoughby's care—Ned, who had grown up with the Starcliffe children and in his youth had wanted to marry her.

Ned was known and loved throughout Orion County for his gentle ministrations. He had always taken care of my grandmother, and when she died, my mother clung to him and he tried to comfort her.

As he told Arthur, she needed more comfort than he realized. She had confided to him that my father had fallen in love with another woman. She kept coming back to Ellsworth Falls all that winter to see him, and in the spring she set up her easel in the meadows along the Belledame. Ned was drawn to her—he admitted it to Arthur. He had an unhappy marriage of his own. And my mother was a beautiful, troubled woman; and once or twice—perhaps more than that—he stopped to sit with her, to share a picnic—"to find out, Arthur, how she was. She was deeply depressed, she hardly saw anyone in the city, she had only this new work of hers and, I suppose, some foolish dream of me."

"Too bad," said Aggie when she heard this story. "I hoped she'd had a bit of a fling." And then she sighed and said remorsefully, "If only we'd known how frightened she was—how frightened of the world."

I set to work restoring my mother's house. I knew the memories that had drawn her to this particular place; I had formed a picture in my head of the peaceful time she would have here when she was well. Neither Arthur nor Flint was pleased with this idea, but when they saw I meant to persist, when they saw the ardor with which I threw myself into the task, they acquiesced.

All during my senior year I drove across the state and camped out in the house by the river. I reshingled the roof and pointed up the bricks and replaced the rotting doors and window frames. Once, lying on my mother's cot and leafing through her books, I felt overwhelmed with loneliness—hers, not mine. I knew I must not fall under its spell, and so I set to work again stripping the stained and blotched wallpaper, hunks of plaster coming away with it, brittle and smooth as bone.

Little by little the house took shape. In the spring I rebuilt an old dry wall; I planted fruit trees; I fought an endless battle with squirrels and mice and muskrats who still did not know the place was no longer theirs.

I made arrangements for furniture from Apple Tree Farm—in storage since the house had been closed—to be sent to the country. I hung the Starcliffe chandelier, the Starcliffe ancestors, the Mary Cassatt painting of the young woman at the piano. I wanted this to be my mother's house, with her beloved things always in view and near at hand.

But she did not get well. A second summer passed and a third, and suddenly I realized that the house would not be hers after all. It was mine.

35

I HAVE LIVED in this house for nearly twenty years. In the late afternoons I sit out in a canvas chair—it is like the chair that Noll designed, the chair in which I felt the thrilling tremors of life in Maude's baby—and I listen to the river going along and watch the birds move to and from the feeder; and if it is spring, I smell the blossoms of the lilacs and the wisteria and the apple trees I have planted in a little field off to the right.

When I take my mother for a drive—she is very old, she is the only one of them left—the roads, the trees, the barns, the fields, the hills are no longer vivid to her. It is as though she were looking through an unfocused microscope. Only a slight adjustment is required—perhaps that is all that is ever required—and yet she cannot manage it.

After I graduated from Harvard I went to work in New York for Arthur. What gripped me so as I climbed the stairs of the IRT and walked the narrow streets with my bag of coffee and Danish, hardly able to contain my anticipation of the day? Why did my heart beat so as I turned the pages of *The Wall Street Journal*? I was like a small boy who has found the first clue in a treasure hunt. The early morning sun made a grid on the plain walls of the bullpen. Only the vapor from my coffee broke the flat golden ingot of light.

I was assigned to two partners, one young and one old; they were my mentors in all things. My responsibilities were clear: I spent thousands of hours at a Marchand calculating machine preparing statistical summaries for the offerings of new securities. When these were completed, my teachers huddled confidingly over the long sheets and explained what the numbers meant. It was like being back in school—and yet there was immense purposefulness about the place. When we met our clients, we were fiendishly well prepared.

I had dinner regularly with Arthur. We had become friends. One evening, a fat folder in his lap and a stiff highball in his hand, he told me the truth about Stim. It took him a long time to spin the story out. At times he stood by the window, staring out over the park with its soft strings of light and patches of darkness; at times he stood by the fireplace and lectured me, which was odd, for he had never lectured me before. His dress, his manner, his furnishings, had been lesson enough.

There was nothing, it seemed, that the Grenfell organization could not find out when it put its mind to it. After my father had married my mother and reneged on his promise, Arthur decided to find out everything he could about Peter Stimson. The Grenfell investigators were to leave no stone unturned. And now I heard it all, feeling horror and rage and sadness, all these things, as the revelations came. My godfather was not an Englishman. There was no record of him at Cambridge. There was no family house in Somerset. He was known to people at Rothschild's and Schroder's, but only on the basis of his American reputation. He was not English, he was German. His name was not Stimson, it was Steinmetz. His father had come to London late in the nineteenth century and worked as a liveryman—he was a drunk, a bully, a thief, and it was in the crueler regions of the city that his son grew up. It was there, when he was six years old, that he had been struck by a carriage and had his right leg amputated, just above the knee.

"Oh, Arthur, I don't think I want to hear it after all."

"I know you loved him—otherwise I would have told you long ago."

He made his way hobbling on crutches. He cleaned stables and emptied slops; he stood sentry on docks while contraband changed hands. It was a time when the archaeological riches of the world were coming to London. Later he would learn how to appropriate some of them for himself. By the age of sixteen, he had learned the rudiments of loan sharking. By the time he was eighteen, he had taken a small step toward respectability. He was a clerk in the bookkeeping department of a small export-import firm, learning about letters of credit, bills of lading. A whole world was opening up. He took more pains with his dress and his speech.

As Arthur's flat voice went on, as he turned the pages of his file, checking it once again for chronological accuracy, I felt my blood chill. "Stop!" I wanted to cry, "Oh, please stop."

And I saw Stim clumping through the kitchen at Apple Tree Farm shouting, "Dear Fräulein!" and Fräulein talking a little German with him. Oh, my mother's preposterous theories! And as the memories came back, I lost the thread of Arthur's voice, I saw only Stim's face staring scornfully at our prim, ruffled ancestors on the wall, and I remembered the warmth of his big bed and the glow of the Ming vases in their dimly lit cabinets and Joseph coming in and out ("In our family the butlers have always been called Joseph, and so of course I had to change his name"), and there swept over me not a wave of revulsion or betrayal but only a deep, immense longing for his arms, for his rough cheeks, for the old days, for the way things had once seemed to be.

In 1914 Stimson and Company was born. In 1915 he bought a run-down house on the North Shore and began fixing it up. In 1919 he hired my father. "He was shrewd about picking young men," said Arthur. "He liked eager country boys with no connections, no money, no chance of finding their way to the distinguished firms. Your father was such a boy."

"But why did he stay, Arthur?"

"He was beholden to him."

Stim had already lent him a little money to help him with the debts of the Kempton Marble Company. When he heard about his engagement and his plans to leave, he offered to help pay off the whole thing—"It wasn't a huge sum," said Arthur, "perhaps fifteen thousand dollars. But to Henry it was a fortune. I knew what that kind of burden could mean. If only he had come to me! But that was exactly what he wished to avoid. I don't suppose I was the most approachable kind of person in those days."

I smiled at the thought of Arthur's approachability.

"In any event, Stimson lent him the money. He gave him a generous raise. He could see the advantages—I hope I am not being unduly vain—of having Arthur Starcliffe's brother-in-law in his employ. Your father was deeply moved. He swore his loyalty to him. And he was never out of Stimson's debt again."

I did not understand how this could be.

"Has your father told you none of this?"

"None."

"Stimson was cruel to him."

But I had seen the two of them with my own eyes—seen them on a summer evening sipping brandy and smoking cigars and talking like old comrades preparing to outwit the world together.

"You don't understand the kind of man this was. He was on the *edge* of things; he was always threatening to back out of deals, trying to improve his hand. And the people around him were speculators, operators, swindlers."

"My father too?"

He fixed me with his stare. I had never seen him so passionate before, so determined to make me understand. And yet it was bewildering.

"I might have said so once. I might have said your father was dishonest. After all, he broke his promise to me. . . . But he was under severe pressure, and it made him take dreadful risks. He speculated in the market. At first I thought he did it the way Flint did, out of a kind of reckless, irresponsible *joy*. But no, it wasn't that. Your father was young, he was impatient and ambitious, but what he wanted most of all was to be free of that first debt to Stim. Unfortunately, he had some bad luck and Stim lent him even more. Stim had him on a string. Sometimes he pulled it in; sometimes he played it out."

"But how long did this go on, Arthur?"

"He gave your father the land for the new house. And he lent him the money to build it, taking a mortgage in return. Don't forget, the house was built in the year you were born. In 1929. And in 1937—people forget that was a dreadful time too—Stim foreclosed. He took the house back from your father and began charging him rent."

"Oh, Arthur!"

"He was one of those men . . . there are certain men who grow up in sordid circumstances who simply cannot resist inflicting a little pain now and then. Charm and generosity, cruelty and pain; that is their pattern. When the war was over and your father was no longer with the firm, when—by God —he was wooing another Kempton, this one my own flesh and blood, I decided I would ruin Stimson." Arthur paused to catch his breath. "And I did."

"And are you glad?"

"Not proud, but yes—glad."

One day the phone in my office rang, and a familiar voice said, "Peter? This is Alexandra."

"Alexandra?"

"Alexandra Moorcock."

"Sandy?"

"I'm in New York. I'm looking for a job. Morley said you were to buy me lunch. At the '21' Club. Do you know it?"

While I was waiting for her, I looked across the room and saw my sister sitting by herself. I went over and said hello.

"Oh, dear," she said, "what are you doing here? I didn't know you came to places like this."

"I don't. I'm meeting a young lady. Is Toby giving you a treat?"

"Not exactly," she said.

I was aware of a figure at my side, an elegant older man in a beautifully tailored double-breasted suit. There was the tangy smell of after-shave, a silk hanky in the breast pocket, a boutonniere.

"Darling," my sister said, "this is Peter."

"Delighted," said the suave gentleman in his nice French accent. "I am François d'Alembert. Your sister and I have been old friends for many years. I do hope you will join us."

"Not on your life," said a willowy young blonde I could not recall ever having seen before. "He's mine."

So Alexandra and I had lunch by ourselves; and so did Susan and François. Afterward my sister told me he had come to America to fetch the poodles and had fetched her instead. "After all," she said, "if Father could marry a countess, why can't I marry a count?"

Arthur was dying. Two or three times a night I would hear his cries and go to his bedroom and pick him up—he weighed nothing by then—and carry him to the library and prop him up with pillows in a sofa or a chair. He would take a sip of brandy and catch his breath and sometimes we would talk. On one of these long, awful nights he looked up at me, flushed, bright-eyed, alert, and said, "I have never told this to anyone before. I would like to tell it to one person before I die. Lord knows, I could never tell your mother. I found some papers, a box of papers."

"I know about the papers, Arthur."

"No, not those papers. They were lost in the fire." He shifted his weight uncomfortably. "These were different papers. I found them in my mother's house after she died. How often I wondered if she had read them—and if she understood. Do you know what they were, Peter? Oh, what a shock it was! Old employment contracts, agreements with the laboratories. My father had withheld them. Do you know what they showed? They showed that those vile, grasping men had justice on their side. My father knew all along that we had no case. I discovered those papers in the winter of 1942. For more than thirty years I had carried the burden of my youthful zeal—and my arrogance. I had forced my father to bring all the documents together, and then the house burned down. And so we lost the suits, and it was all my fault! Imagine what it meant, discovering that we would have lost *anyway*. And he never said a word! He was a great inventor, but not always a great man—it was a most useful discovery, although I must say it came a bit late."

It was this final revelation of Arthur's that forced me, at

last, to try to come to terms with my own father. I did not want to find him—as Arthur had found his—when it was too late. I had avoided and scorned my father before my mother's illness; afterward I could not help but add the blame for it to the list of his offenses. On a rare visit to the Georgetown house, so transparent was my animosity that Maude took me aside in the library and demanded to know why I was so *hard*. My father didn't deserve it. He didn't deserve to be hated by a second son.

The word shocked me, for it was the one Susan had used years before to chastise Randolph, and for the very same reason. And yet, when my father and Maude moved abroad, I seldom answered their letters. Even Arthur's tale about Stim had not softened me, for I was too busy trying to digest the story on my own terms, measuring my own sense of hurt and betrayal. I couldn't reconcile Stim's affectionate, comforting presence—the countless times he had hugged me, the exhilaration of our cruise together—with the man in Arthur's dossier.

But when Arthur told me of my grandfather's papers, I felt an unexpected welling up of despair, as though a lesson I had already learned must be learned again. I discarded my own losses and turned to my father, lest he be added to the list. And I was a small boy again waiting at the Clarkstown station. The trains come in, one after another, shuddering and spouting cinders, and then I hear Tony say, "Eesa here," and there he is, coming across the platform, his gait heavy, his face lined with worry and fatigue. I feel again the fleeting touch of his cheek as he bends quickly to kiss me and hand me his briefcase and the evening papers. I feel the sting of the ball as he drives it at me so fiercely in the gathering summer dusk. I am alone in my room, and I hear the anger in his voice as he and my mother begin quarreling. And at last I begin to understand the harm that Stim has done and how it has spread through our lives, building on the harm that came before, the injuries that are sustained in our youth and which in our pride and ignorance we cannot reveal or share.

I began to write my father after that. And he immediately wrote me back—long, discursive letters about his travels abroad, all in a surprisingly awkward hand.

After Arthur died, I left Grenfell, Starcliffe and Company and went to architectural school to learn about houses. And after I had learned what I thought I wanted to know, I discovered it was not houses that interested me so much as their settings—the clasp of vines and the flow of paths and the great bulk and shadow of trees.

That is why when I come now to the Dome and look down upon the valley, there are so many places familiar to me. I have helped make some of them. I have made ponds and moved walls and laid out gardens.

Yet it is the other places—the ones in which I have had no hand—that are inscribed in my very being. The chimneys still rising from a green jungle where my grandfather's house once stood; the cottage where one summer evening my father came across a lawn to greet my mother for the first time; the old quarry; the Grover School; the graveyard where they are buried, Clarence and Lila, Flint and Arthur, Randolph.

My Aunt Agatha is not buried here. One afternoon she climbed the steps to the dress circle of Carnegie Hall and closed her eyes during a performance, and she did not wake up again. She is buried in the next valley, near Emma and Millard Kempton.

My father rests in a foreign land. For twenty years he and Maude traveled the world; and wherever they were, he wrote, telling me of the bridges and power plants and steel mills he was helping to build. At times I thought he sounded more like an engineer than a banker. I wrote back, about my marriage and the birth of my daughter, about my new career and my life in the valley. Toward the end of his life, I went with an elegant Frenchwoman—my sister, Susan, holding a pair of poodles on a bright-red leather leash—to visit him at St. Paul-de-Vence. We found an old, white-haired man puttering in a pleasant garden in the Mediterranean sun.

Sometimes in the autumn I come up here early in the morning. There is no mist at this time of year; the air is like crystal. The plowed fields, the stone walls, the steeples, the lovely barns—how courtly they are. Like an old engraving. It is when I take the farther view that I realize again how deceptive our surfaces are. The fine facades of houses, the mild tilled fields—they seem so secure. And yet on all sides is forest. The vines and creepers come; they will hold the houses in their embrace again. In the darkness of the woods stone walls topple. Boulders come from the earth and push their way through the soil and thrust themselves against gravestones whose inscriptions have already been worn soft by the winds of time. So even there we are not wholly safe. We leave and we return and we are laid to rest. Our constructions are fragile, our premises false. There is only movement, only change, and the ceaseless flow of charged particles trapped for a moment and breaking free.

ABOUT THE AUTHOR

WINTHROP KNOWLTON is Director of the Center for Business and Government at the John F. Kennedy School of Government at Harvard University and a Public Service Professor at the School. He was for a time partner in the investment firm of White, Weld & Co. and President of the New York City Ballet. He has published two nonfiction books and coauthored a thriller.